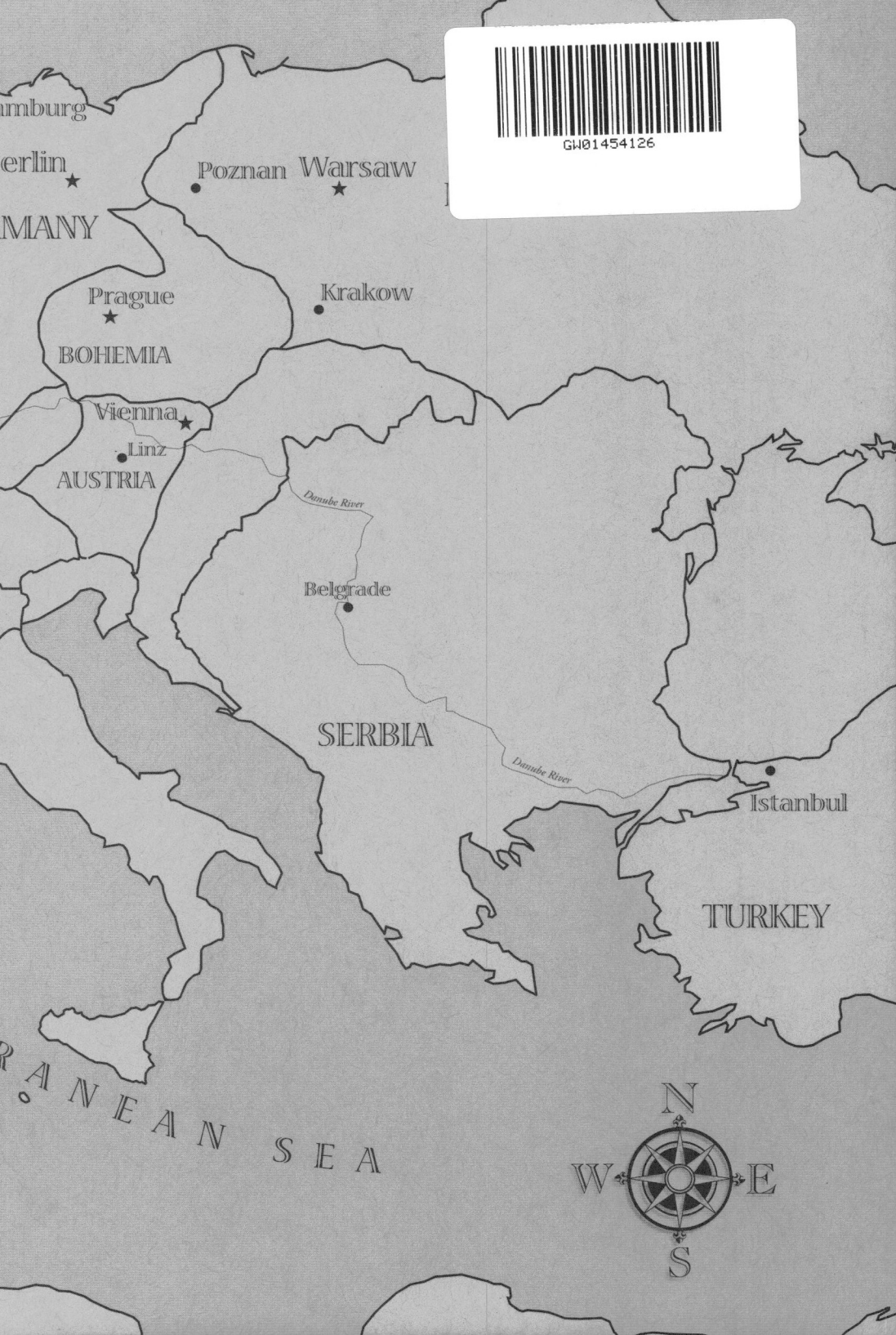

THE
STRASBOURG
SAGA

# Scandal in

Published by
Me'sorah Publications, ltd

# Amsterdam

## AVNER GOLD

FIRST EDITION
*First Impression … September 2008*

Published and Distributed by
**MESORAH PUBLICATIONS, LTD.**
4401 Second Avenue / Brooklyn, N.Y 11232

*Distributed in Europe by*
**LEHMANNS**
Unit E, Viking Business Park
Rolling Mill Road
Jarow, Tyne & Wear, NE32 3DP
England

*Distributed in Australia and New Zealand by*
**GOLDS WORLDS OF JUDAICA**
3-13 William Street
Balaclava, Melbourne 3183
Victoria, Australia

*Distributed in Israel by*
**SIFRIATI / A. GITLER — BOOKS**
6 Hayarkon Street
Bnei Brak 51127

*Distributed in South Africa by*
**KOLLEL BOOKSHOP**
Ivy Common
105 William Road
Norwood 2192, Johannesburg, South Africa

Typography by CompuScribe at ArtScroll Studios, Ltd.

Printed in the United States of America by Noble Book Press Corp.
Bound by Sefercraft, Quality Bookbinders, Ltd., Brooklyn N.Y. 11232

# CONTENTS

# Scandal in Amsterdam

# AUTHOR'S NOTE

ALTHOUGH TWENTY YEARS ELAPSED between the publication of *The Marrano Prince* and the recently published *The Long Road to Freedom*, its immediate sequel, it was very gratifying to me that my readers are still engrossed in the story of the Strasbourg family and all the colorful characters who inhabit their world. The excitement of so many readers who rejoiced that their beloved saga had been revived was more than I could have expected. I only hope that they find the new offerings as satisfying as the earlier ones.

*Scandal in Amsterdam* is the first of the books that does not feature Rabbi Shlomo Strasbourg, the celebrated rabbi of Pulichev; the saga will return to him in future books. In this book, we follow the fortunes of the Dominguez family as they arrive in Amsterdam and make the acquaintance of the mischievously wise Rabbi Mordechai Strasbourg, one of the rabbis of the Ashkenazi community of Amsterdam, and his son Amos, who befriends Sebastian Dominguez.

The story takes place in the late seventeenth century, when the Dutch Republic controlled a vast colonial empire and dominated the international economy. The Republic had the world's largest fleet of merchant ships and the first modern stock and commodities exchanges. It was the wealthiest nation in the world, not because of its natural resources, but because of its genius for business and commerce. The greatest resource of the Dutch Republic was its people, who excelled at business and finance. A disproportionate number of these people were Jewish.

In the beginning of the seventeenth century, groups of wealthy ex-Marranos who had escaped from Portugal and Spain made their way to Amsterdam and established a small community. Since most ex-Marranos were Portuguese-speaking, the community came to be known as the Naçao, the Portuguese Nation. By the end of the century, the Naçao was a large and vigorous community that flourished in the atmosphere of religious tolerance and economic vitality that characterized Amsterdam during that period, known as its Golden Age. The Naçao contributed greatly to its success.

The Portuguese community during this time was led by Rabbi Yitzchak Aboab da Fonseca, and its principal yeshivah, Etz Chaim, was headed by Rabbi Yaakov Sasportas, famous for his courageous opposition to the messianic claims of Shabbesai Tzvi. Both of these rabbis make cameo appearances in the book.

There was also an Ashkenazi community in Amsterdam, known as the Tudescos, which means "Germans" in Portuguese. Most of the Tudescos who came to Amsterdam were refugees from the Cossack massacres in Poland and Ukraine and from the German states where they had been subjected to relentless persecution and expulsions. The Tudescos were more numerous than the Portuguese, but they were much poorer. Some of them engaged in business and finance, but most were craftsmen, peddlers or recipients of charity.

The relations between the two communities were cordial on the surface, but tensions simmered underneath. These tensions would burst into the open years later when a Sabbatean adventurer named Nechemiah Chayun arrived in Amsterdam and caused a rift between the Portuguese leadership and Rabbi Tzvi Ashkenazi, known as the Chacham Tzvi, the rabbi of the Tudesco community. That unfortunate episode will be described in a future book.

Since the Strasbourg Saga is a work of historical fiction, the stories feature interaction between historical characters and fictional characters. The distinction is not always self-evident to the reader, and therefore, I would like to identify the characters who are historical; all the others are fictional.

In the previous book, *The Long Road to Freedom*, the historical characters are: King Louis XIV of France; Queen Marie Thérèse of France; Minister Jean Baptiste Colbert; Emperor Leopold I of the Holy Roman Empire; Leopold Karl von Kollonitsch, Bishop of Wiener Neustadt; Count Reudiger; Charles Léopold Nicolas de Vaudemont, Duke of Lorraine; Prince Waldek; Cardinal Pentucci; Sultan Mohammed IV of Turkey; Grand Vizier Kara Mustafa; and King Jan Sobieski of Poland. There is also a character called Hannibal the Dwarf. However, while history records that the Queen of France was attended by dwarfs, it does not record their names. The name Hannibal is my own invention.

The historical characters in this book are: Rabbi Yitzchak Aboab da Fonseca, rabbi of the Portuguese community of Amsterdam; Rabbi Yaakov Sasportas, *rosh midrash* of Yeshivah Etz Chaim; King Louis XIV of France; and Minister Jean Baptiste Colbert. Hannibal the Dwarf also makes an appearance.

In the next book, the scene shifts to Colonial America, where the growth of the European settlements, not even a century old, has already put them on a collision course with the numerous Indian nations that surround them. Tiny Jewish communities are taking root in some of these colonies. The opportunities are enormous, but so are the dangers and the challenges.

A.G.
Lakewood, NJ.
15 Elul 5768 (2008)

# SAFE PASSAGE · 1

S EBASTIAN SAW THE ORANGE MUZZLE flashes before he actually heard the shots. Bullets whizzed by his ear as he leaped from the saddle and ran for cover. The shots were coming from a thick stand of pines alongside a rise in the road ahead. He looked over his shoulder and saw that Gonzalo was right behind him, running toward the trees in a zigzag pattern.

Sebastian and Gonzalo had chosen to return from Vienna to Metz in Lorraine by an overland route. It would have been easier to go by riverboat most of the way, but speed was all-important. Doña Angelica, Sebastian's mother, was in trouble, and a delay of even several days could be critical. Their route took them through the wooded mountains of the Black Forest in Baden-Württemberg in southwestern Germany, after which it would be just a short run to Strasbourg and on to Metz. But now, on a deserted stretch of road far from any town, they had been ambushed.

The two men crouched in the shadows of the wooded roadside, watching the pines from which the shots had been fired. There were no signs of movement, no more muzzle flashes, no more shots. Gonzalo primed a pair of pistols and jammed them into his belt. Meanwhile, the horses remained on the road where they had been abandoned, rolling their eyes and stamping on the ground.

"I'm going to get the horses, Gonzalo," said Sebastian. "Look how skittish they are. If we leave them there, they might just bolt and run all the way back to Villingen, and then what are we going to do? Walk to Strasbourg?"

"I suppose you're right," said Gonzalo. "But stay low to the ground, grab just one horse and use it as a shield as you bring it here. Let's hope the other horse follows you."

Sebastian crouched at the edge of the trees like a runner preparing for a race. He cast one final glance toward the stand of pines, and then he sprinted toward the horses. Instantly, a new volley of shots erupted. Sebastian dove to the ground and covered his head with his arms. A dozen paces ahead he could see the horses rear up in terror. The horses turned back in the direction from which they had come. They galloped at break-neck speed down the road and then disappeared into the cover of the woods in which Sebastian and Gonzalo were hiding.

Sebastian jumped to his feet and raced back toward the woods, expecting a new volley of shots at any moment, but none came. He reached the safety of the woods gasping for breath. His face was covered in a cold sweat. Gonzalo was leaning against a tree, a pistol in each hand.

"It looks like we lost our horses," said Gonzalo. He did not look particularly distraught. "We'll figure something out. At least, you didn't get hit."

"I don't think we lost the horses, Gonzalo," said Sebastian. "I saw them run into the woods, a short way down the road. They're on this side of the road, so I think we can reach them without exposing ourselves to any more musket fire. We'll just stay in the woods."

"All right. Let's go, but be careful. What's the plan?"

"First, we have to get the horses and secure them so they don't run away. Otherwise, we'll be stranded here in the middle of the Black Forest. Then we backtrack through the woods until we reach those pines up ahead. If we are very careful, we can come around behind the shooters and trap them. Who do you think they are?"

"I don't know, Don Sebastian. They may be ordinary highwaymen out to rob us, although this is not how highwaymen operate. They might be assassins sent by the same people who betrayed you to the authorities in Vienna. It may even be a case of mistaken identity."

"Not very likely, Gonzalo. Let's go."

Gonzalo shoved his pistols back into his waistband, and the two men plunged into the woods in search of the horses. They fought their way through underbrush and climbed over dead and rotting tree trunks that had fallen onto the forest floor. They strained their ears for the sounds of the horses, but all they heard were the sounds of birds chattering in the trees and the howl of wolves in the distance.

Presently, they came to a small brook. Off to the right, they could just get a glimpse of the road, but straight ahead they saw only the tangle of shadows and vegetation. They exchanged glances and pushed ahead.

Soon, they found the first signs of the horses. Small branches were freshly broken, and here and there, they could make out hoofprints in the soft mulch of the forest floor. The horses seemed to be headed deeper into the woods. They would not go far. Once their panic dissipated, they would stop and wander about in bewilderment.

Suddenly, they heard the frightened whinny of a horse. The men broke into a run along the trail left by the horses. Gonzalo pulled one of his pistols and held it at the ready in case it was a snake that had frightened the horse. In less than a minute, they saw the horses. But it was not a snake that had frightened them. It was a man dressed completely in black.

The man was untying Sebastian's saddlebags from his saddle. He slung the saddlebags over his shoulder and ran into the woods in the direction of the road.

"Stop!" shouted Gonzalo. "Stop or I'll shoot."

The fleeing bandit paid Gonzalo's warning no heed. He ran as quickly as the thick underbrush would allow, and the two men gave chase.

Carrying the saddlebags on his shoulders, the bandit was at a disadvantage. The bags were unwieldy and they often got tangled in the branches, causing the bandit to lose precious moments as his two pursuers gained steadily on him. In desperation, he reached down to a sheath strapped onto his leg and pulled out a dagger. Then he spun around and hurled the dagger at Gonzalo. The dagger whooshed through the air and imbedded itself into a tree trunk not far from where Gonzalo's head had been a moment before.

Meanwhile, Gonzalo had instinctively dropped to his knees to avoid the missile and fired one of his pistols at the bandit. The bandit's sharp cry of pain signaled that he had been hit, but he continued his flight, leaving behind a trail of blood.

Gonzalo and Sebastian did not delude themselves into thinking that their quarry was no longer dangerous. A wounded quarry is sometimes the most dangerous of all.

"Let's split up," said Gonzalo. "I'll follow the trail of blood, and you circle around to the right to catch him if he tries to reach the road before I get to him."

"Good idea."

Sebastian grabbed a stout fallen branch, which he could use as a cudgel or to smash through tangled underbrush. After he disappeared into the woods, Gonzalo set off in pursuit of the wounded bandit. The trail of blood led in a wide arc turning toward the right, in the general direction of the road. Gonzalo walked slowly and carefully, checking constantly to see if the trail turned into the shadowy woods where the pursued might be lying in ambush for the pursuer.

After a few minutes of tracking, he saw the bandit lying face down near a fallen oak in a small clearing. The stolen saddlebags lay on the ground a few paces from where the bandit lay. There was a ragged hole in the bandit's lower back, and a puddle of blood was pooling on the ground beside him. The man appeared to be dead.

Gonzalo thrust his unfired pistol into his belt and approached the body warily. As he reached out to grab the bandit and turn him over, the bandit rolled over on his own power, and his right hand came up with a pistol pointed directly at Gonzalo's face. Gonzalo reeled back and turned his shoulder, bracing himself for the impact of the bullet. But before the bandit could fire the pistol, it was flung into the air when Sebastian's cudgel struck him on the wrist from below. The bandit fell back to the ground clutching his wrist and groaning in agony.

Sebastian stepped out into the clearing.

"Gonzalo," he said in a tone of mock disappointment, "after all those hunting trips to Asturias, I thought you were an experienced tracker. Since when do you let your quarry catch you by surprise?"

"All right, all right. You saved my life. I owe you."

"No, you don't." Sebastian looked down at the bandit writhing on the ground. "I think we should have a word with this fellow."

"Absolutely," said Gonzalo.

He took a flask of water from his belt and crouched down beside the wounded bandit.

"Would like a drink of water?" said Gonzalo.

The bandit nodded. Gonzalo undid the opening of the flask and poured a little water into the bandit's mouth.

"What's your name?" asked Gonzalo.

The bandit turned his head away and refused to speak.

"Listen, my friend, said Gonzalo. "There's no point in keeping secrets any more. You're on your way to a better world. Why not make your last moments on this beautiful earth pleasant and friendly? Would you like another drink?"

The bandit nodded again, and Gonzalo gave him another small drink.

"So let's try again," said Gonzalo. "My name is Gonzalo Sanchez. What's yours?"

"Gunther. Gunther Schultz."

"Pleased to make your acquaintance, Gunther. It's a pity we have to meet under such circumstances. So how many of you are there, you know, you and your friends up in the pines?"

The bandit coughed, and a trickle of blood ran down his chin.

"How many, Gunther?" said Gonzalo. "It was a nasty thing that you and your friends were trying to do. After all, what did we do to you or anyone else for that matter? Tell us what we need to know, and you can leave this world with a clear conscience, Gunther. So how many?"

"Three."

"You and two others?"

"Y-yes ... w-water."

Gonzalo gave him another drink.

"Why did you try to steal those saddlebags?"

The bandit coughed and spit up some more blood.

"Gunther, my friend," said Gonzalo, "why the saddle-bags?"

"Karl ... he told me ... cold ... feel ... cold."

"Who's Karl? Is that your leader?"

"Leader ... yes ... cold."

"What is Karl's last name, Gunther?"

"Karl ... Karl ... cold."

The bandit shivered once, and then he lay still. Gonzalo put his finger to the bandit's neck. There was no pulse.

"He's gone," he said.

"We'll have to bury him," said Sebastian. "We can't very well leave a body to rot in the forest. He may be a criminal, but he is still a human being, made in the image of the Lord. And then we'll have to check out those pines to see if his friends are still waiting in ambush."

"They're gone for now, I'm pretty sure of it. But we'll still have to be extra careful the rest of the way. They may lay a trap for us anywhere on the road. It's a pity that old Gunther didn't tell us much before he departed for a better world."

"Well, he did tell us something," said Sebastian. "He told us that there are two more of them and that one of them is named Karl."

Gonzalo grimaced. "Not much to go on."

"I wonder why he wanted my saddlebags."

"What's in those saddlebags, Don Sebastian?"

"Not much. Do you think they waylaid us for my saddlebags?"

"It's possible, I suppose. If they heard there was something of value in it."

"It would have to be something of great value," said Sebastian, "to have three bandits lay an ambush and shoot at us."

"So what's in the saddlebags?"

Sebastian shrugged. "Some clothing. My *tefillin*. A siddur, you know, a Jewish prayer book. Not much else. Nothing of any real value to a bandit."

"Let's take a look," said Gonzalo.

They emptied the saddlebags and spread its contents on the ground.

"What's this?" said Gonzalo as he pulled an envelope out of a folded shirt. The heavy paper of the envelope was richly grained. It was not sealed.

"It's our safe passage. The one King Jan Sobieski sent to me before we left Vienna. I mentioned it to you."

"You did, but I've never seen it. What does it say?"

Sebastian pulled a single sheet of paper from the envelope and unfolded it. The royal seal of Poland was stamped at the top of the sheet.

"Here, I'll read it to you," said Sebastian. "It goes as follows, 'This safe passage, issued on the authority of the Holy Father in Rome, as represented by Cardinal Pentucci, the papal legate, and on the authority of the Crown of Poland, as represented by us, is for the protection of Don Sebastian Dominguez, all members of his family and all his attendants and agents. He and they are to be given safe passage and extended every courtesy and consideration at all times. He and they are under our protection, and we take full responsibility for their safety and welfare. This safe passage also bears testimony to their having received full pardon and amnesty for any and all ecclesiastical and secular charges that have been levied against them in all the domains of Christendom. Signed, Jan Sobieski, King of Poland.' That's the whole thing."

"There's not much a bandit could do with that piece of paper," said Gonzalo, "unless he changed his name to Sebastian Dominguez."

"I suppose not. But that paper is extremely valuable to us. What if they tried to steal the letter because they didn't want us to have it?"

Gonzalo scratched his chin. "So you think this whole ambush was just to distract us so that they could steal the letter? Who would want to do such a thing?"

"The same someone who betrayed me to the authorities in Vienna as a fugitive from the Inquisition. Someone wants to harm me, and I don't know who it is. He failed in Vienna, thanks to Rabbi Strasbourg's intervention with the King of Poland, so now he is trying to steal my safe passage and strip me of my protection."

"But why steal the safe passage?" said Gonzalo. "Why not just shoot us both to death? They could have done it."

"Maybe this mysterious someone just wants to harm me. Maybe he doesn't want to go so far as to kill me dead."

"You think he doesn't want to kill you, this mysterious someone? Don Sebastian, if the King of Poland hadn't come to your rescue at the last moment in Vienna, you would have been on your way back to Madrid for a rendezvous with a stake and a pile of burning firewood. The way I see it, that is serious killing."

Sebastian shook his head. "You're asking a good question, Gonzalo. I don't know the answer."

# TRIALS AND
# TRIBULATIONS · 2

RAIN FELL OVER THE CITY OF METZ in dense sheets obscuring the last traces of a dingy twilight as the weary travelers stabled their horses. Gonzalo immediately went off to his lodgings in a rooming house just inside the Jewish quarter, and Sebastian headed for the house the Dominguez family called home until they could find a more permanent home in Amsterdam.

During all the interminable, bone-crunching hours in the saddle on the way back from Vienna, the plight of his mother was never far from Sebastian's thoughts. He had been told that she had been accused of witchcraft and was in deep trouble, but nothing more. And now, as he walked along the dark cobblestoned streets, eyes downcast, just minutes away from seeing his mother, he was almost oblivious to the rain.

Try as he might, he could not imagine what in the world could be at the bottom of this ridiculous accusation. Was it completely fabricated? Or was it a horrendous distortion of something factual? Would there be a trial? *Heaven help us*, he thought, *is it possible that my mother escaped the Inquisition just to be tortured and burned at the stake as a witch?*

He looked up and saw that he had reached his destination. He took a deep breath and knocked on the door. There was no immediate answer. His heart pounding, he knocked again, this time harder. Presently, the door was opened by Helga, the housekeeper. When she saw Sebastian standing on the doorstep, she caught her breath, and her eyes widened with shock. But she recovered her composure quickly and gave him her customary dour look.

"Good evening, sir," she mumbled. "You mother and brother are in the parlor. May I take your coat? I will bring you a towel and tell Madame that you are here."

Sebastian dried his hands and face, but before he could join his family in the parlor, his younger brother Felipe came running out to greet him.

"Sebastian!" Felipe cried out. "You're alive!"

The brothers embraced for several long moments, shedding hot tears on each other's shoulders.

"Thank the Almighty," breathed Felipe. "Oh, thank the Almighty. I cannot thank Him enough that you're back. How did you get away from prison in Vienna? It must have been a miracle."

"It's a long story, Felipe. There'll be time for it later. The main thing is I'm free and safe. That's more than I can say for Mother. What's happening here?"

"We are desperate, Sebastian. Desperate! But first, come inside. Mother twisted her ankle, and she couldn't come out here to see you. But she is waiting anxiously to see you. She never thought she'd see you alive again."

"I'm coming," said Sebastian. "Just give me a moment to take off my boots and put on a pair of clean slippers."

"Giscard Duvalier is here, too," said Felipe. "He's trying to help us. I don't know where he finds the patience to deal with our problems."

"He's Mother's cousin. Kinfolk are loyal to each other."

"Well, maybe sometimes," Felipe conceded. "But he's a count, a member of the French aristocracy, and we've publicly declared ourselves to be Jews. Our family ties have been broken, from both sides. I mean, he has nothing to gain by helping us, and I'm sure the association with us is unpleasant for him."

"Then perhaps he's helping us out of habit," said Sebastian as he struggled to pull off his sodden, mud-splattered boots. "Our families have been close for many years — no, for many generations — and now that we're moving apart, this is his gracious farewell. Let's take advantage of it." The boots finally came off, and he pulled on the slippers. 'Let's go in. I don't want to keep Mother waiting."

Doña Angelica burst into tears when she saw Sebastian. She buried her face in her hands and wept until her shoulders trembled from the effort. Sebastian shook hands solemnly with Giscard, who had risen to greet him. They waited silently until Doña Angelica finally regained her composure.

She smiled ruefully at Sebastian. "A fine homecoming party we've prepared for you, haven't we? Here we were beside ourselves with worry that you might be sent back to Spain, Heaven protect us, and now you're free and home. We should be dancing for joy, but instead … How did you get away?"

"Rabbi Strasbourg persuaded the King of Poland to set me free. It's a long story. I'll tell you about it later. What's happening with you is more important."

"We have a terrible problem, Sebastian. It's just awful."

"We'll deal with it, Mother," said Sebastian. "With the help of the Almighty, we'll get through this, but first you have to tell me what is going on. They told me in Vienna that you've been accused of witchcraft. Is that true?"

"I've been accused," said Doña Angelica.

"So it's true," said Sebastian.

"But I'm no witch!" she added fiercely.

"Of course not, Mother. Perish the thought."

"Utterly preposterous," added Giscard. "What an outrageous thought!"

"Can just tell me what happened, Mother?" said Sebastian. "I'm completely in the dark."

"It was all so innocent, so innocent," said Doña Angelica. "Who could have thought it would come to this? Carolina had a few mishaps, one after the other, so Frau Klinger — the matchmaker, remember her? — she said it was the evil eye."

"The evil eye," Sebastian repeated.

"That's right. That's what she said. What do I know about these things? All I knew was that Carolina had nearly been killed by a runaway horse and that her ankle was swollen to twice the size. Then she faints, and then she gets a rash. Frau Klinger is an experienced Jewish woman, and she said it was an *ayin hara*, an evil eye. She said it's in the Torah and the Talmud, so who am I to argue? She said that when some people saw how happy and radiant Carolina was and what a good match she had made, they became jealous and gave her the evil eye. And she also said these things would keep happening to her unless we did something about it."

"Did something about it," Sebastian repeated.

"That's right. She said we had to get rid of the evil eye."

"So how did you get rid of the evil eye?"

"She did something called *bleigiessen*," said Doña Angelica. "She poured hot lead into a pan of cold water over Carolina's head again and again until it stopped forming recognizable shapes and came out as a single clump. She also said some prayers while she was doing it."

"And this was supposed to take away the evil eye?" said Sebastian.

Doña Angelica nodded. Giscard squirmed and looked away.

"Did it help?" said Sebastian.

Doña Angelica shrugged. "Nothing happened to Carolina after she did it. You remember her wedding in Hamburg. Wasn't it beautiful? Everything went so smoothly, and she now has a wonderful husband. Would anything have happened without this lead business? How would I know?"

"All right. Where did you do this thing?"

"Here. In the kitchen."

"Where was I?"

"You were away."

"And Felipe?"

"You were both in Strasbourg."

"And Helga the Norwegian saw you. That's what I was told in Vienna."

"That's right. She was supposed to be sleeping, but she heard noises and came downstairs to investigate. She saw us."

"And she reported you?"

"Yes."

Sebastian bristled. "So why is she still here?"

"It's not her fault, Sebastian. She's just an ignorant, stupid woman. She saw these peculiar things going on, and she didn't know what to make of it. And besides, it wouldn't look good for me to send her away while this was going on. It would look like a confession of guilt."

"Yes, that was my suggestion," said Giscard. "I strongly advised against sending her away."

"So she reported it," continued Doña Angelica. "And it wasn't right away. It was on her conscience a long time, and finally, her priest pulled it out of her during confession. The priest reported it to the authorities, and they started an investigation. Then — "

"I think that's enough, Mother," Felipe interrupted her. "It's too much of a strain for you to tell the rest of the story."

"Yes, absolutely," said Giscard. "I can take over from here, madame."

"Would you be so kind?" said Doña Angelica. She leaned back with a sigh of relief and dabbed at her forehead with a lace handkerchief.

"Of course, madame," said Giscard. "Well, let me see now. So much has happened, Sebastian. Let me see. Well, your mother sent me a message as soon as she realized she was in trouble. That was an excellent response. Exactly what she should have done under the circumstances. So I came to Metz and arranged a meeting with the magistrate in charge of the case. First, I impressed on him that Madame Dominguez was a kinswoman of the royal family of France and that she was under the protection of His Royal Majesty, King Louis XIV."

"But that was not enough?"

"Well, yes and … It certainly gave him pause and stopped him from issuing a warrant for your mother's arrest pending trial. But it did not persuade him to drop the case entirely. It seems there are powerful people advising him to push forward with the prosecution."

"So what happens now?"

"I hired Monsieur Jean-Marie Cartier, one of the best lawyers in Paris, to represent Madame Dominguez and —"

"I want to pay his fees," Sebastian interrupted. "It is unconscionable that you should keep bearing our expenses."

"My dear boy," said Giscard, "I don't know what to do with all the money I have. If I don't bear these expenses, I will have even more money at my disposal. And what will I do then?"

Sebastian responded with a half-hearted smile and said nothing.

"In any case, the lawyer believes that the case against Madame Dominguez is very weak and that he will have no difficulty demolishing it at trial."

Sebastian sat forward. "Trial! Are you saying that my mother is going to be put on trial? Is there nothing we can do to spare her that ordeal?"

"It's even worse than that," said Felipe. "If we go to trial, there's no telling what the result will be. No matter what the lawyer from Paris says. And don't forget these unnamed people who are pushing the magistrate to take the case to trial. These are our enemies. They may even be the same people — or person — who betrayed you to the authorities in Vienna. Who know to what lengths they will go in order to get a guilty verdict?"

Sebastian blanched. He looked at Giscard with fear in his eyes. "So is that where we are? Is that the situation? We have to prepare for a trial and hope for the best?"

"Yes and no. We have to prepare for trial, because there is a good chance that it is going to happen. Although Heaven help us if it does. But we also have to explore other routes. I am trying to get an audience for Madame Dominguez with His Majesty the King. If we can get him to hear us and give us his support, we should be safe. In the meantime, we press forward as if we are going to trial."

"Do you think the King will grant us an audience?"

"I don't know. It is not even three months since the Queen died, and I believe the King is still officially in mourning. Will he be inclined to grant Madame Dominguez an audience? I don't know. And even if he is, will he be inclined to do so during his mourning period? I don't know. And even if he is, will he be inclined to come to her assistance? I don't know. These are big questions. Unfortunately, I don't know the answers."

"I see," said Sebastian. "So we have to think seriously about a trial."

"Well … I'm afraid so. In the meantime, I've hired two private detectives to investigate the source of the pressure on the magistrate to take the case to trial."

"And have you gotten any reports yet?"

"Actually, I have," said Giscard. "The pressure is coming from two high government officials who appear to have come into substantial sums of money recently. There is also a priest pressing the magistrate for a trial, but we have discovered no indications that he is being put up to it. It may just be religious zeal for him. He's an old man, and he remembers the great witch trials of thirty or forty years ago. Many hundreds of witches were burned at the stake in those days, and he was very much involved in those cases as a young monk. But witch trials are much more of a rarity these days. Perhaps he is nostalgic for the old days and sees in this case an opportunity to turn back the clock and recapture some of the old excitement."

Sebastian shuddered. "How about the other two?"

"It seems fairly certain that the government officials involved have been paid off to bring pressure on the magistrate."

"Do we know by whom?"

"I'm afraid not. All we've discovered so far is that they've had meetings with an unidentified stranger who may or may not be an agent for wealthy foreigners. My investigators have reason to believe that the money is coming from a foreign source, but they have not come even close to identifying the source."

"Can we discredit them by proving that they've taken bribes?"

"And how are you going to do that, my dear boy? Pardon me for calling you a boy when you're all of thirty years old already. It's just force of habit."

Sebastian brushed it away with a wave of his hand.

"So as I was saying," said Giscard, "you cannot prove anything. I mean, just because a man suddenly has a windfall of money, does that prove he came by it in some illegal manner? Does it prove that he is corrupt? Why should a man have to explain how he got money that he has in his possession? If someone wants to accuse him of wrongdoing, let him prove it. There are no witnesses and no proof that we can take to the magistrate."

"How about the magistrate himself?" said Sebastian. "Has he been paid off as well? If he was, we haven't a chance in the world if we go to trial."

"To be honest with you, my dear ... Sebastian, I don't know. The thought has crossed my mind, too. My investigators are looking into it, but so far they haven't come up with anything on the magistrate. I've spent the last two weeks in Metz, and I must head back to Paris early tomorrow morning."

"And what are we to do?" asked Sebastian. "I mean, do you have any constructive suggestions for us while we wait for the axe to fall?"

"It might be worthwhile to spend some time praying in the synagogue. Other than that, there is not much you can do. I'll leave you the names of my agents here in Metz, so you can stay in touch with them in case there are any developments and if you want up-to-date information. I don't know when I'll be coming back here again, but you can always send me a message, directly or through my agents, and if I can help you, I will." He stood up and reached for his cape. "I must be on my way. I regret I couldn't be the bearer of better news."

"We're grateful for everything you're doing for us, Giscard," said Doña Angelica. "May the Almighty bless you and protect you. But before you go, what do you think? How will this whole thing end? What's going to happen to me?"

"Madame, I'm sorry to say that I haven't the faintest idea."

For the next two weeks, Doña Angelica, Sebastian and Felipe met often with the investigators and the agents of Giscard Duvalier, but they made little progress. Sebastian told them the good news about the money Don Pedro had left them, but money was of little interest to them when their mother's very future was in question.

They also made a special trip to Paris to meet with Monsieur Jean-Marie Cartier, the lawyer Giscard had retained. They took rooms near the Rue Parmentier, not far from where they had lived when they first left Spain. The following morning, they met with the lawyer.

"I wouldn't worry too much, Madame Dominguez," said the lawyer. He was thin as a skeleton, and his teeth were yellow. But his eyes were sharp and intelligent, and they never stopped moving.

"We could certainly use some reassurance," she replied.

The lawyer smiled at her. "Then you've come to the right place. My staff has done some excellent research, and I feel confident that we would win at trial, if it should ever come to that. Would you like to hear the outlines of my case?"

"Of course, we would," said Sebastian. "And we would also like to decide if we are comfortable with it."

"Oho!" said the lawyer. "I hope you are not going to be difficult clients. You have to trust me. So! The outlines of the case?"

"Yes," said Doña Angelica. "Please."

"Very well." The lawyer rested his elbows on his writing table and steepled his fingers. "Here it is in a nutshell. According to my research, witchcraft or sorcery comes in basically two forms. One, the casting of spells to coerce people into certain states or to do certain things. Two, conjuring up the spirits of the dead as a way of learning what the future will bring. Therefore, performing a ritual for the purpose of removing some form of spell that had been cast by others is essentially a defensive action against witchcraft. It is not witchcraft itself."

The lawyer unsteepled his fingers and leaned back in his chair.

"That's it?" said Sebastian.

The lawyer nodded. "That's it. Quite brilliant, don't you think?"

"No doubt," said Sebastian. He was quaking inside. "But

couldn't someone possibly argue that a spell of any kind is witchcraft, even if it is in defense against another spell?"

"Someone could conceivably argue that, but it is a poor argument. My reasoning is impeccable and persuasive."

"But you are conceding that the concept of the evil eye is a sorcerer's spell when it is nothing of the sort. And you are conceding that the removal of the evil eye is also a form of a spell but that it is not witchcraft since it is being performed in self-defense, when it is also nothing of the sort. Isn't that true?"

"My dear sir," said the lawyer, "do not presume to teach me my business. It is not for nothing that I am one of the most sought-after lawyers in Paris."

"Do you have a high rate of acquittals, M. Cartier?" said Sebastian.

"The highest."

"How many of your clients are acquitted? I mean, how many out of every ten."

The lawyer stroked his bony chin. "At least seven. Maybe eight."

"M. Cartier, could we rethink the case and meet again tomorrow?" said Doña Angelica in a conciliatory tone. "Perhaps you can think of something even more brilliant. Your strategy may gain an acquittal for me, but it will not defend my honor. I am not a witch, monsieur, and I have never done anything even remotely resembling witchcraft. Perhaps, monsieur, we can come up with a plan that secures my freedom and also defends my honor."

"Of course, madame," said the lawyer. "I will review the case and devise a different strategy."

Doña Angelica wept in the carriage on the way back to their lodgings for the night. If the family had entertained any hope that the trial could be decided in her favor, the visit to the lawyer had dispelled it. Sebastian and Felipe tried to reassure her, but their words were hollow and unconvincing.

There was a message from Giscard waiting for them at the station of the concierge. He asked that they remain in Paris for another four days. He wanted to meet with them, but he would be unable to manage before then.

They made arrangements to remain in Paris over Shabbos. There were a number of Jews living in Paris, even though Jews were officially barred from all of France. Having once lived in Paris, Doña Angelica knew where to find kosher food. There was also a prayer group that met in a private apartment not far from their hotel. They would manage.

As it turned out, they enjoyed a serene and beautiful Shabbos, just the three of them together. They put thoughts of their misery out of their minds and focused on the holy atmosphere of Shabbos. Doña Angelica prepared the meals while the men went off to pray. Although meager by the standards of home, they enjoyed the food and the wine, accompanied by the traditional *zemiros* and other songs, as if it were the most sumptuous of feasts. Felipe, who was becoming quite the Torah scholar, regaled his mother and brother with inspiring insights into the weekly portion and stories from the Midrash. Afterward, they talked about their experiences in their new environment, their memories, especially of Don Pedro, and their hopes and aspirations for the future. They did not acknowledge that there might not be much of a future. At that moment, they felt very close to the Almighty, and they trusted that He would not abandon them.

Early Sunday afternoon, Giscard came to their hotel. His face was more flushed than usual.

"I have news, Madame," he said.

"Good news, I hope," she replied.

"Well, … yes, I suppose. The King has agreed to grant you an audience. You are to come to Versailles with both your sons and no one else."

"You mean no rabbis?"

"Exactly. Last time you came with Rabbi Mendel Strasbourg. This time, I was told specifically that he is not invited, nor is any other rabbi. It was the Queen who had asked for him last time. She had questions, if you recall. And by all counts, they were answered to the satisfaction of Their Majesties. But the Queen has gone to Heaven, may she rest in peace, and the King has no interest in having discussions with rabbis."

"I quite understand. When are we to come to Versailles?"

"Well, last week they told me that the King would see you in January, but this morning a messenger from the Palace informed me that the audience has been moved up to tomorrow at noon."

"Tomorrow!" said Doña Angelica. "But I have nothing to wear! All I brought with me from Metz are traveling clothes."

"Do not distress yourself, Madame," said Giscard. "My wife will send over a number of outfits and accessories later, along with her seamstress to make any necessary alterations and her personal maid. You will not be shamed."

"Giscard, how can I ever thank you and your lovely wife? You think of everything. We would be lost without your help."

"Think nothing of it, Madame. His Majesty has expressed a desire to have me present at the audience as well, and of course, it will be my great honor to attend. I will come by with my carriage tomorrow morning. We should leave quite early to make sure we are there with plenty of time to spare. Better a little too early than a little too late, I always say."

"Indeed," said Sebastian. "Monsieur, when my mother asked you if the news was good, there was a moment's hesitation. And then you responded with a lukewarm yes. What was the reason for your hesitation? In what way could this be anything other than good news?"

Giscard glanced at Doña Angelica and then turned away. He cleared his throat twice before he looked at Sebastian, and he did not meet his eyes.

"Well … it's like this, Sebastian," he said at last. "I hope and pray that everything goes well at the audience with the King tomorrow. But if, Heaven forbid, it doesn't … um … ahem … if the King … turns you away …" His voice trailed away for a while. Then he squared his shoulders and continued. "But who needs to dwell on negative thoughts, right?"

"I need to dwell on negative thoughts, monsieur," said Sebastian. "I need to confront our problems with open eyes. What happens if he turns us away?"

"Yes, please tell us," said Doña Angelica.

"Very well, madame," said Giscard. "It's not good, I'm afraid. If the King rejects your petition, any chance you had of gaining an acquittal at trial will be diminished. The rejection of your petition will surely be entered as evidence against you, and it would be quite damning."

The color drained from Doña Angelica's face. "That is terrible," she breathed.

"So what can we do?" asked Sebastian.

"I believe we can do nothing," said Felipe. "We have no choice but to appear once the audience has been granted. Isn't that so, monsieur?"

"That is so," said Giscard.

"Then we have to go and do our best," said Felipe. "And we have to pray to the Almighty that we find favor with the King."

The following morning, Giscard's lavish carriage was at their hotel not long after dawn. It was the third time the carriage had come to their hotel in the previous twenty-four hours. The night before it had brought Madame Duvalier's seamstress and personal maid, and they had spent several hours preparing Doña Angelica for the audience.

They arrived in Versailles with over two hours to spare, but by the time they had gone through the official process preliminary to a royal audience, their waiting time was much reduced. At exactly five minutes after noon, they were escorted into the royal audience chamber. The King was seated on a throne. He looked relaxed. His minister of finance, Jean Baptiste Colbert, stood at his right side. Hannibal, the dwarf favored by the late Queen, stood to his left; the dwarf was dressed completely in bright red, head to toe. A single empty chair stood facing him about ten paces away.

Doña Angelica, her sons and Giscard Duvalier bowed deeply before the King.

"Madame Dominguez," said Colbert in a toneless voice, "out of deference to you, a lady and a royal kinswoman, His Majesty has granted you permission to sit in his presence. The chair is for you."

Doña Angelica recognized these words as almost exactly the ones he had spoken on the occasion of her previous audience. She bowed and sat without comment. In the presence of the King, one only spoke in response to a question.

"Madame Dominguez, we cannot say that we are pleased to see you again," said the King. "Certainly not under these circumstances. Very few of our Christian kinsmen demand so much of our personal attention. Indeed, now that fate has saddled me with a Jewish kinswoman, it has also saddled us with her problems. And such problems! Lead pouring? Sorcery? Is there any truth to these charges, madame?"

"Absolutely none, Your Majesty," she replied. "It was just an innocent Jewish custom to counteract the effects of jealousy and ill will. Your Majesty surely knows that Judaism utterly forbids sorcery, and that was the furthest thing from my mind."

"Your Majesty," said Colbert. "I am told that the ritual of *bleigiessen* is used by the peasants in Germany on New Year's Day to divine what the future will bring. That would seem to be a form of sorcery."

"Your Majesty," said Doña Angelica passionately. "I have no idea about what goes on with the peasants in Germany on New Year's Day. All I know is that we were not trying to perform any sort of divination. We were just trying to protect my young daughter from the jealousy and ill will of those who could not bear to see her enjoy radiant health and good fortune."

"No doubt," said the King. He looked at Giscard. "And how about you, Monsieur le Comte? We are seeing a lot of you lately because of our common association with our Jewish kinswoman. Quite awkward. But your loyalty and gallantry are certainly admirable. You are obviously on her side in this matter, but we still want to hear what you have to say on the matter."

"It is my honor, Your Majesty. I have known Madame Dominguez for many years. Ever since she was a child. She is an intelligent, levelheaded, gracious woman. If she would only embrace Christianity, she would glitter at the royal court. She is no witch, Your Majesty. I would stake my life on it."

The King looked to Colbert on his right. "Monsieur le Ministre, what have you to say on the issue in general?"

"Your Majesty," said Colbert, "we have not had many witch trials in France for quite a few years. Ever since the power of the Church went into decline, the number of witch trials was greatly reduced. Should Madame Dominguez be arrested and tried as a witch, it would be a highly publicized event, more so if she were to be condemned and burned at the stake. It would not bring honor to the Crown, especially since it incidentally publicizes the blood relationship between the Jewish defendant and the royal family."

"No, we don't want that," said the King.

"Also, it would damage the relationship of the Crown with the leading Jewish financiers of Europe, who would undoubtedly view the trial as an attack on the Jewish people."

"So you are saying that we should issue a royal order that all charges against Madame Dominguez be dismissed?"

"Not quite, Your Majesty. There is another side to this. If there were to be a royal decree of that sort regarding a case that is being actively prosecuted, there will be questions asked. Why would the King come to the defense of this woman? Once again, the blood relationship would be publicized. And there may also be objection to the special favor shown to a Jewish woman accused of witchcraft. People may wonder why this woman was spared the judicial process, which presumably conducts fair trials for all defendants. Why should the truth not be determined by a duly constituted court of law?"

"So you are saying I should not issue the decree?" said the King.

"I am simply saying, Your Majesty, that there are positives and negatives on both sides of the question."

"So what would you advise?"

"In case of doubt, it is sometimes better to do nothing and hope for the best."

Sebastian listened to this exchange with growing desperation. If the King did nothing, his mother would be forced to go to trial, and if it were revealed at the trial that there had been an audience and that the King had declined to help, the chances of acquittal would shrink to almost none. He was on the edge of panic when he had a sudden flash of an idea. He cleared his throat to gain the King's attention before he reached a decision.

"Your Majesty, may I say something?" he said.

The King looked at him, as if surprised that he had spoken.

"You are Sebastian Dominguez, I believe, the older son."

"Yes, Your Majesty."

"Do you have something of value to add to this discussion? We are willing to listen to suggestions."

Sebastian reached into his pocket for the envelope he had received from Jan Sobieski, which he always carried on his person. "I believe this may offer a solution, Your Majesty."

"We shall see." He turned to the dwarf standing to his left. "Hannibal, make yourself useful. Take the paper and read it for us."

The dwarf stepped forward and took the paper from Sebastian. He puffed up his chest, and in a deep baritone, he read aloud the Polish king's safe passage for the Dominguez family. When he finished, he offered the paper to the King, but when the King waved it off, he returned it to Sebastian.

"So what is your thought?" said the King. "You realize, of course, that we are not happy with the King of Poland, whom we once considered a good friend of France. We did not send troops to defend Vienna because the Austrian Empire is our enemy, but the Polish king did more than join the defense of the city. He delivered them a brilliant victory. But go ahead. We are listening."

"Your Majesty," said Sebastian, "the safe pardon specifically states that we are under his protection and that he takes full responsibility for our safety and welfare. That means that this trial is going against the specific wishes of the Polish king and is an affront to his crown. It is, therefore, a case of *lèse majesté*, an offense against the sovereign power in a state, even though it concerns a foreign monarch. As long as Your Majesty does not issue an order that contradicts this safe passage, my mother can be released from trial based on the safe passage alone. Your Majesty need not get involved."

The King pursed his lips and looked at Colbert. "What do you say?"

Colbert nodded his head gravely. "It makes sense, Your Majesty. I can have the Ministry issue the order canceling the case, and Your Majesty need not be connected with it in any way."

"Then that is what we will do," said the King. "Madame Dominguez, you may thank your son for his quick thinking. You are free to go. The trial will be canceled. Monsieur Colbert will see to it right away. It is our understanding that you are relocating to the Portuguese community of Amsterdam. Nothing stands in your way now. We wish you good fortune. And without meaning to be rude to a kinswoman, albeit a Jewish one, we hope that we have seen the last of you."

# THE WELCOMING PARTY · 3

AMSTERDAM IN THE WINTER was a cold and frosty city, but to the Dominguez family it was like being in paradise. It was the most vibrant Jewish city in all of Europe. Nowhere else did Jewish people enjoy as much freedom, privilege and opportunity as they did in Amsterdam. This was the place where the family would start a new life as proud Jews. This was the place where they would build a future far more glorious and lasting than anything they could have anticipated as secret Jews living in Spain.

The Dominguez family had followed a well-beaten path to the capital of the Dutch Republic, situated in the province of Holland in the Netherlands. A century earlier, the United Provinces of the Netherlands, the northern part of the country, had broken away from the Spanish Empire. At the same time, they had also cast off the yoke of the Catholic Church and declared a policy of religious tolerance. Although the policy was intended to benefit the Dutch Reformed Church and other Protestant denominations, it had also been extended to the Jewish faith, and a strong Jewish community had sprung up in the Dutch cities.

On the evening of their arrival in Amsterdam, there was a knock on the door of their rented cottage at the very edge of the Jewish Quarter. Helga opened the door and saw three men dressed in the resplendent attire favored by Portuguese Jews in Amsterdam. One of them wore a suit of crimson brocade, while the other two wore suits of different shades of bright blue. All three wore felt hats with enormous brims adorned by multicolored feathers.

"Is this the home of the Dominguez family?" the man in the crimson suit asked in rapid Portuguese.

The only word Helga appeared to understand was the name Dominguez. She nodded her head and replied in halting French, "*Oui, monsieur. Ici c'est maison de la famille Dominguez.*"

"*Dites-leur que nous voudrions parler avec eux,*" he said. "Tell them we would like to speak with them."

"*Certainment, monsieur,*" said Helga. She gave them a sour look and went off to find Doña Angelica.

Five minutes later, the family and the three visitors were gathered in a small sitting room in the front of the house, where a couch and two armchairs stood out like small islands in a sea of unopened bundles. Three more chairs had been brought in from the kitchen and were squeezed in among the bundles.

The man in crimson remained standing while the others sat down. He was older than his two companions, short and squat, with a minuscule white beard and an unmistakable air of authority. "Señora Dominguez," he began in Spanish, "we have come to welcome you and your family to Amsterdam. The three of us are members of the Maamad, which is the ruling council of the Naçao, the Nation, as we Jews of the Portuguese community here in Amsterdam call ourselves. By the way, is it all right for us to speak in Portuguese?"

"*Certamente, nós todos falamos Português,*" she said. "Of course, we all speak Portuguese. Please speak in the language of your greatest comfort."

"*Muito obrigado, senhora,*" the man in crimson said, this time speaking in Portuguese. "First, let us introduce ourselves. I am Eduardo Colon. My two colleagues are Senhor Yakob

Santos and Senhor Martino Vega. We are called *parnassim*, which means leaders in Hebrew. That is our responsibility, to provide leadership for the community. Believe me, senhora, it is a heavy burden."

"I have no doubt that it is."

"Yes. We have to make sure that the synagogue is properly maintained, that the kosher laws are properly observed by all the merchants and vendors, that the charity funds are properly collected and distributed, that the behavior of our people conforms to the proper customs and standards of our community as well as many other duties and obligations. One of our most pleasant duties is to welcome new arrivals to our community, especially new arrivals as distinguished and celebrated as your family. We offer you our condolences on the tragic yet heroic death of your husband, may he rest in peace, and we hope that the time of troubles for your family has come to an end. We will certainly do everything in our power to ensure that you find yourselves well-situated here."

"Thank you so much, Senhor Colon," said Doña Angelica. "You are really very kind. I can see that we will really enjoy Amsterdam. And Senhor Colon, it is not necessary for you to stand while you speak. We would all be pleased if you would sit down, and we can continue this pleasant conversation in a more informal manner."

Eduardo Colon bowed from the waist and sat down.

"Before we talk about practical matters," he said, "and before we answer your questions — and I am sure you have many of them — I think it would be helpful if we told you a little about our city and our community. I would like my friend Senhor Yakob Santos to do the honors. Yakob?"

Yakob Santos was a nondescript man of about forty. He leaned forward and placed his palms on his knees.

"If you will indulge me, senhora," he began. He nodded at Sebastian and Felipe and added, "*E cavalheiros*. Amsterdam is really something of a miracle for us. In 1492, when our people were expelled from Spain, most of them went to Portugal or to one of the Muslim lands, such as Turkey and Morocco. But a few made their way here to Amsterdam, which was little more than a small town in one of the Spanish possessions. Their number was small, and there was hardly any community to speak of for a very long time. Do you know a little about the history of the Dutch Republic?"

They all nodded.

"Then you know that the united provinces of the north revolted against the Spanish crown and declared a republic in 1581, almost exactly one hundred years ago, and they made it an official policy that all religions should be tolerated. The word got around that secret Jews could emigrate from Spain and Portugal to the Dutch Republic and find safety, security and a pretty good chance for prosperity, and many people took advantage of this opportunity. One of them was my great-grandfather Senhor Santito Santos. That's what he was called in Toledo. When he came to Amsterdam in 1593, he became Shmuel, and my family has used only Hebrew names ever since, even though most Portuguese Jews use Portuguese names. In the five generations that we've been here in Amsterdam, we've seen this city become the richest in all of Europe. At first, there were hundreds of us, and now there are thousands. Our community has contributed greatly to the success of the city, and of course, we have also benefited greatly."

"We are very pleased to be here in Amsterdam," said Sebastian. "It is our dream come true. My father's dream come true, although he is not here to see it. But really, for those Marranos who wanted to leave Spain and come out into the open as proud Jews, was there really nowhere else to go but Amsterdam?"

"That is an excellent question, Senhor Dominguez," said

Yakob Santos. "But if you think about it, where were they to go? The only real option was to go to Turkey or perhaps one of the other Muslim lands, but that was not so appealing to most Marranos who were accustomed to the European culture and spoke only the European languages. So what did that leave us? The ghetto in Venice? The German states with their persistent and unpredictable expulsions, where you never knew from one year to another where you would be bringing up your children? Poland and the countries of the east where Jews were persecuted, despised and restricted in their opportunities to earn a livelihood? France and England where Jews were forbidden to live? The Americas, North and South, where Spain and Portugal ruled most of the colonies and the Inquisition was as active as in Europe? Which of these places was so appealing?"

"Not many," conceded Sebastian.

"No, not many. So most Marranos just chose to stay where they were and take their chances. They concealed their Jewishness. They ate pork in public and attended church on Sundays, and they hoped for the best. Anyway, Amsterdam was the answer to our prayers, and it has been true to its promise. We have flourished here. We've built synagogues. Massive ones. Wait till you see the Portuguese Sephardic Synagogue. It is magnificent. Majestic! And we've built schools and *yeshivot*."

He paused for a moment to scratch his neck. Sebastian was immediately on guard. He had long ago learned that when someone scratched his neck while speaking it was a sign of discomfort. Something untrue or unpleasant was probably coming.

"The credit for everything that has been accomplished," continued Santos in a solemn voice, "goes to the rabbis and the early members of the Maamad. The three of us take no credit for our own efforts. We are merely following in the footsteps of great men, and it is our mission to preserve their important work. We are the guardians of the community, and we are obligated to use every means at our disposal to preserve the well-being of the community, spiritual and material."

"So what is your point?" asked Sebastian.

"And what do you mean by every means at your disposal?" added Felipe.

Doña Angelica gave her two sons a look, as if to chastise them for their belligerence, but she made no comment.

"Well, I was trying to say," said Santos, "that … ahem … you will … "

"It is best to be blunt, Yakob," said the third *parnas*, the one named Martino Vega. He looked like a droopy-eyed owl and spoke in a high-pitched voice. "I will answer both questions to the point. Yakob is being especially delicate and diplomatic out of respect to your family, but it is important that we are very clear. It is our duty as members of the Maamad to lead the community in the name of the rabbis, and as such, we have been given the power of issuing a *cherem* when we feel there is a need to do so."

"A *cherem*?" asked Doña Angelica. "That sounds like a Hebrew word, but I've never heard it before. What does it mean?"

"It is a decree of excommunication," said Martino Vega. "If we feel that someone has violated the laws and customs of our community or has somehow undermined the welfare of the community, it is in our power to excommunicate the guilty person. Sometimes, the *cherem* is for a specific period of time, and sometimes it is forever. Once we place a person under *cherem*, no one in the community is permitted to speak with him or have any dealings with him whatsoever for the entire duration of the *cherem*. We try to use it as seldom as possible, but we do use it from time to time. It makes people pause and think twice before doing something that is not approved by the community."

Doña Angelica shuddered. Sebastian and Felipe just sat there stone-faced.

Eduardo Colon motioned to Vega to be still.

"Believe me, it is not our intention to frighten you, senhora," said Colon. "Or to disturb you in any way. We just feel that it is important to let new arrivals know how things work in our community. Let me just give you one example. Almost thirty years ago, there was a fellow in our community named Benedicto Spinoza. He was a quiet fellow but very bright, and he had these wild notions about the Almighty and the world that went against everything we believe. In other words, he was an *apikores*, a heretic of the worst kind."

"I believe I have heard the name," said Doña Angelica.

"It is quite possible," said Colon. "The man is dead now, but it was quite a scandal in its time. The rabbis of the community, including Rabbi Isaac Aboab da Fonseca, may he live and be well, who was already our chief rabbi at that time, brought Spinoza before a rabbinical court and questioned him. They didn't want to put him in *cherem*, especially because his father was a respected member of the community, but they had to do something to keep him from spreading his insidious ideas. They offered him money to be quiet, but he insisted on mocking our holy Torah, so they put him into *cherem* and saved the purity of community."

"That is very interesting," said Sebastian. "But what does it have to do with us. Are you warning us not to spread heresy?"

"Of course not," said Colon. "This was just an extreme example of the *cherem* that I thought you should know about."

"And did the rabbis put Spinoza in *cherem*?" asked Felipe. "Or did the Maamad?"

"Oh, it was the rabbis," said Colon. "Absolutely. It was the rabbis. The Maamad could never have dealt with such a case. No, the Maamad deals with smaller offenses. If a member of the community is seen to be fraternizing with gentiles not for the purpose of business, he is called before the Maamad and warned. If a member of the community is seen to be eating food that is not kosher or frequenting the taverns of the gentiles or behaving in other ways that are forbidden by our holy Torah, he is called before the Maamad. And very important, if a member of the community is known to have behaved unethically in the conduct of business with other members of the community, he is called before the Maamad. In all cases, he is given a fair hearing, and if he is found guilty, he is given a warning, sometimes two. But if he is persistent in his improper behavior, then we are left with no choice. He forces us to put him into *cherem*. That is our system here in Amsterdam, and it works."

"I'm sure it does," said Sebastian. "So what is your purpose in telling us about this? Are you concerned that one of us will run afoul of the Maamad?"

Colon recoiled in feigned shock. "Heaven forbid! We have come here to welcome you to Amsterdam and to offer you our assistance in any way we can. But while we were here, we wanted to explain to you how are system works."

"Thank you so much, senhor," said Doña Angelica. "It was very kind of you to come. And certainly very interesting." She stood up. "As you can see, we have not even unpacked yet or rested properly from our journey. I'm afraid I will have to step away. If you wish to speak some more with my sons, then by all means do so. Good day, gentlemen."

The three *parnassim* jumped to their feet.

"Our most humble apologies, senhora," said Colon. "It was not our intention to inconvenience you. We will be on our way. And once again, we extend to you our warmest welcome to Amsterdam and our best wishes for your success and good fortune."

They all bowed to Doña Angelica and shook the hands of Sebastian and Felipe, and then they were gone.

As soon as the door closed behind them, Doña Angelica sat back down on the couch.

"So what did you think of that, my children?" she asked, slipping back into the more familiar Spanish language.

"I think they're harmless," said Felipe.

"And you, Sebastian?" said Doña Angelica. "What do you think?"

"I don't know. I suppose I agree with Felipe. I don't really believe that all three of them pay a visit to every new arrival. It may usually be just one of them or one of their underlings. But they may think that, as blood relatives of the royal families of Spain and France, we needed an additional warning."

"A lot of good those relations would do us," said Doña Angelica. "You heard King Louis. He hopes he's seen the last of us. Our former relatives are not much interested in a Jewish family living in Amsterdam."

"Oh, I think they understand that as well, Mother," said Sebastian. "It's just that we might think ourselves in a class of our own. Which we don't, of course."

"Of course," said Doña Angelica.

"Of course," echoed Felipe.

"So let's forget about this little interlude. I don't think we will have any problems with the Maamad. After all, why should we? Let's talk about the money Father left us."

"I have a lot to do, Sebastian," said Doña Angelica. "Don't get me involved in money matters. I would much rather leave it to you men."

"I'm not going to get you involved, Mother," said Sebastian. "I just want to tell you and Felipe what I intend to do, and if you have any comments, please tell them to me."

"All right," said Doña Angelica.

Sebastian pulled his chair a little closer and leaned forward. "As you know, Father left us letters of credit in the sum of one hundred thousand Reichsthalers, which is the same as one hundred and fifty thousand Dutch guilders. Tomorrow morning, I am going to go to the Bank of Amsterdam and open up accounts for all of us. For you, Mother, there will be thirty thousand guilders. For Carolina and Felipe, fifteen thousand each. That is a lot of money, because a person can live very handsomely on three thousand guilders a year."

He paused to let them do the arithmetic in their heads.

"That leaves ninety thousand guilders in my name. That is how Father wanted it, as long as I took upon myself the responsibility of supporting and caring for the family. As I told Don Alejandro in Vienna, the responsibility would be mine even if Father had left no money for us."

Doña Angelica smiled at him. "You are a good son, Sebastian. You're just like your father. Thank you for telling this to us."

"Wait, I'm not finished. Of this money, I intend to give nine thousand to charity. I also intend to give Gonzalo two thousand guilders to purchase a tavern and a small house. And of course, we will need a house, so I am earmarking five thousand guilders for that, which leaves me about seventy thousand guilders for commerce. According to my information, this amount could bring us a very comfortable living if I invest it wisely, which I intend to do."

"Everyone intends to invest wisely, Sebastian," said Felipe, "even those who don't actually do it."

Sebastian smiled. "Perhaps I should have said that I intend to invest it conservatively. With such a large sum, there will be no need to take risks."

Doña Angelica stood up. "So everything is resolved. I really feel that better times await us here in Amsterdam. This place is just a larger, more exciting version of the Portuguese community in Metz. We had no problems there, and we won't have any problems here. Now, I suggest we all go to sleep. I don't know about the two of you, but I, for one, am completely exhausted."

Fifteen minutes later, a dark figure detached itself from the shadows of an alley across the way from the silent cottage in which the Dominguez family slept. Another dark figure detached itself from the shadows of the trees on the other side of the cottage. The two figures came together for a few moments of whispered conversation. Then the second figure returned to the shadows of the trees, and the first figure slipped away into the night.

# RABBIS AND BANKERS · 4

ARLY THE NEXT MORNING, Sebastian and Felipe had a
long walk to the Portuguese Synagogue from their
rented cottage eastward all the way across Vlooyenburg, the
artificially constructed island in the Amstel River on which
most of the Jewish community was located.

They passed clusters of ships with teams of stevedores
unloading their wares. They crossed canals on which river-
craft ferried passengers and merchandise. Once they had to
wait while the bridge across a canal opened like a drawbridge
to allow a sailing ship to pass through.

As they neared the heart of the Jewish community, they
passed stately brick homes with charming gables and front
stoops swept clean by white-capped maids. They saw many
men and boys emerging from their homes and walking eastward in the direction of the synagogue. They turned right
onto a wide street identified by a sign on one of the buildings
as St. Antoniesbreestraat. Then they crossed the Houtgracht,
the last canal before the synagogue, and continued on the
Jodenbreestraat, the Jews' Broad Street, past a large open-air
market just beginning to stir, and on to the synagogue on the
Muiderstraat.

After prayers, many people came over to welcome the new
arrivals and wish them good fortune. Eduardo Colon, wearing a yellow suit and resembling a canary with a white beard,
waited until the crowd had lessened. Then he led the two

brothers to the front of the synagogue where the rabbi was sitting in an upholstered armchair and looking into a *sefer*. Preoccupied with his learning and his thoughts, the rabbi did not immediately see the two newcomers. Colon put a finger to his lips to signal that they wait in silence.

Felipe knew all about the rabbi, and he watched him in fascination. Rabbi Isaac Aboab, a descendant and namesake of the fourteenth-century author of *Menoras Hamaor*, was born in Portugal in 1605 to a Marrano family. He came to Amsterdam at the age of seven, not even knowing he was Jewish until then, and by the age of eighteen, he had become one of the junior rabbis of the city. In 1642, he had become the rabbi of the Dutch colony of Pernambuco in Brazil, but when the Portuguese captured it, he returned to Amsterdam and became its chief rabbi. Rabbi Aboab was a living example that greatness could be achieved even from humble beginnings, and Felipe aspired to follow his example.

Unlike the rabbi, Felipe had not really known authentic Jewish life and Torah study until he was almost twenty years old, but during his days in Paris and Metz, when Rabbi Mendel Strasbourg had introduced him to the Talmud, he had fallen in love with its grandeur and brilliance. Although he had said nothing to his mother and brother, a secret ambition had grown in his heart. He wanted to become a rabbi, not so much to lead a congregation but to learn the highways and byways of the vast world of the Talmud. If his family thought he would seek to learn a profession or to engage in commerce in Amsterdam, that was not what he wanted. It was not the booming commodities exchange that attracted him to Amsterdam but rather its distinguished rabbis and excellent *yeshivos*. And now he would have the opportunity to meet the illustrious Rabbi Aboab.

As if sensing Felipe's thoughts, the rabbi suddenly raised his eyes and looked directly at Felipe. The rabbi was close to eighty years old. His face was gaunt and wrinkled, with an aquiline nose and cheeks like shadowy caves beneath his cheekbones. His beard was full and white as snow, and his *peyos* framed his face like two billowing white clouds that completely obscured his ears. But most striking were his eyes, deep, intense, passionate. He looked like an eagle with a skullcap perched across his forehead.

The rabbi paid no attention to Eduardo Colon or Sebastian. He just stared at Felipe without saying a word. Felipe felt as if the rabbi's eyes were penetrating to his very soul. He felt his heart beat faster and his face become flushed. Panic rose up in his throat. He wanted to turn and flee, but he was riveted to the floor, pinned down by the rabbi's intense gaze. He gasped for breath, and the rabbi's eagle eyes were suddenly transformed into bottomless pools of kindness.

The rabbi turned to Colon with a question in his eyes.

Colon stepped forward. "I would like to introduce two new members of our community to the rabbi. This is Sebastian Dominguez and this is his younger brother Felipe. Their father, Don Pedro, gave up his soul to sanctify the Name of the Almighty at the stake in Madrid three and a half years ago."

The rabbi nodded. "Who has not heard of Don Pedro Dominguez?" he said, his voice cracking with the fatigue of age. "Welcome to Amsterdam. What do you intend to do here once you are settled?"

"I was considering doing business on the commodities exchange," said Sebastian. "Our father left us a modest amount of money, which I would like to invest. Perhaps the rabbi could give me a blessing for success."

The rabbi closed his eyes for a moment before he responded. "May the Almighty bless your efforts, and may He keep and protect you from your enemies in the merit of your holy father."

Sebastian paled at the rabbi's unexpected blessing, but he bent over and kissed the rabbi's hand without saying a word.

The rabbi turned to Felipe. "You are not interested in commerce, are you, my son?" he said. "What fire burns in your heart?"

Felipe caught his breath. "I want to overcome my ignorance," he said. "I love the Torah. When I sit with a page of Gemara in front of me, when I look into the commentaries of Rashi, the Tosafists and others, when I look at what Rambam and the Shulchan Aruch say, I am like a child standing before the most exquisite painting. I feel its beauty and magnificence, but I do not understand it. And I have this feeling that … that … if I could somehow understand it, I would be very close to the Almighty."

The rabbi's face broke into a broad smile, and his eyes danced with delight. He reached out and embraced Felipe.

"You will find what you seek, my son," he said. "You will understand, and you will help others understand. You will fill your mind and soul and heart with the holy knowledge, and you will share it with others and illuminate their lives. Go straight from here to the Etz Chaim Yeshivah. Senhor Colon will tell you exactly where it is. Tell Rabbi Yakob Sasportas, the *rosh midrash*, that he should take you under his wing. Starting with a good breakfast."

Felipe was beside himself with joy as he and Sebastian left the synagogue. Eduardo Colon had given him the exact directions, and it turned out that the yeshivah was little more than a stone's throw away.

"Are you sure it's all right with you, Sebastian?" he said. "I know we were planning to go to the bank together. I was actually looking forward to the experience. I've never been in a bank. But this is … Are you sure it's all right if you go without me?"

Sebastian felt a twinge of jealousy at his brother's excitement. The prospect of buying and selling on the exchange did not really excite him, certainly not in the way that going to meet Rabbi Sasportas was exciting Felipe. His younger brother had found the spark that would illuminate his own life and the lives of others, as the rabbi had said. He knew where to find his inspiration, and the rabbi had sensed it in him even before he had spoken a word. But Sebastian had not taken to the study of Torah in the same way that Felipe had. He had grown up as a soldier, a *caballero* more comfortable in the saddle than in the study hall. Where would he find his inspiration? Where would he find the kind of inspiration, he thought, that Rabbi Shlomo Strasbourg had described to him in Vienna? Where would he find the inspiration that would infuse every moment of his life with meaning and importance?

"Don't worry about it, Felipe," he said as he patted his brother on the back. "I can handle a bank manager by myself. You go to the yeshivah. Later, I'll tell you about the bank, and you can tell me about the yeshivah. I'll wager that what you'll have to say will be far more interesting than what I will."

"I hope so," said Felipe. "And make sure you tell Mother that they're giving me breakfast here."

They walked together to the building that housed the yeshivah. Sebastian waited until Felipe went inside, then he turned and walked home by himself.

An hour later, he was on his way to the bank. He wore a dark gray suit of heavy wool with an embroidered lace collar and a large black hat with one orange ostrich feather that ran the length of one side of the brim and hung over the edge behind him. The suit had a specially enlarged inside breast pocket, in which he was now carrying the letters of credit he had brought from Metz. He also carried a pouch on a long strap slung over his left shoulder in which he carried four large biscuits, a chunk of cheese and a piece of lead pipe.

It was a typically frigid January day in Amsterdam, bone-chilling but not quite cold enough for snow or ice to form. The air was clear and crisp, and Sebastian quickened his step with anticipation. A new life awaited him. He was not as excited about the commodities exchange as Felipe was about joining the yeshivah. But it definitely promised to be an interesting experience. Perhaps it would capture his imagination. And even if it didn't, it would undoubtedly broaden his knowledge and understanding of the world. Perhaps it would be the first step in the journey that would lead him to his personal destiny.

A man in a woolen cap pulled low over his eyes and a sailor's jacket with the collar turned up stood in front of a flower shop, partially blocking the way so that the passersby should pay him attention.

"Fresh flowers," he was calling out. "Hothouse orchids, tulips and roses just cut this morning. Special January prices."

As Sebastian stepped to the right to walk around him, the man swung his forearm against Sebastian's left shoulder and sent him sprawling into the alleyway beside the flower shop. Sebastian struggled to his feet, but another man who had been standing in the alley grabbed him in a bear hug from behind, pinning his arms at his side.

"Get the pouch, Karl," the second man shouted.

The man in the woolen cap reached for the pouch and grabbed it by its strap. Sebastian clamped his left arm over the pouch and held it tightly against his side. At the same time, he lifted his right foot and slammed it down heel first on the instep of the man holding him from behind. The man screamed in pain and released him. Sebastian ripped the pouch from the man in the woolen cap, spun around and slammed it against the side of the other man's head. The lead pipe in the pouch made a dull thud as it struck home, and the man fell to the ground clutching his ear.

Sebastian was about to spin back to face his other assailant when a sudden blow to his lower back made him cringe
with pain. The man in the woolen cap had punched him
in the kidney, but Sebastian did not allow that to stop him.
Gritting his teeth against the pain, he turned and went into a
defensive crouch, but the man in the woolen cap had moved
to the side. He kicked out at Sebastian striking him in the
knee and knocking him off his feet. His hat flew off his head
and landed in a puddle against the wall.

Meanwhile, the other man was shaking his head to clear
it and trying to get to his feet.

"Get the pouch, Karl," he shouted in guttural German.
"Get the pouch."

The man in the woolen cap grabbed the pouch, but
Sebastian held on to the strap with an iron grip. As they struggled, Sebastian reached out and pulled the woolen cap off
Karl's head. The man was completely bald with a jagged scar
running down the middle of his bare scalp. His eyes were the
palest blue, almost colorless, and they seethed with hatred.

A knife suddenly appeared in Karl's hand. The blade
flashed in the sunlight, and Sebastian backed away, looking
for an avenue of escape. The alleyway behind him was blocked
by a locked door from which emanated the stench of spoiled
fish. The only way out into the nearby street was blocked by
an angry assailant with a nasty knife in his hand. The other
man had regained his balance and was looming behind.

Sebastian looked around for a weapon. He saw a chipped
earthenware plate that had been discarded, and he grabbed
it in his right hand as he backed away. In his left hand, he
gripped the strap of the pouch, ready to swing it as a mace.
Karl lunged forward, the hand holding the knife extended.
Sebastian immediately sent the plate spinning toward him
like an athlete throwing a discus. Karl ducked, but the man
behind him did not have the presence of mind to do the

same. The plate struck him in the jaw, and he went down like a felled tree.

Even while his accomplice was falling to the ground, Karl lunged forward again. This time, Sebastian swung the pouch at his extended arm, and Karl managed to pull it back just before the pouch struck him. Karl went into a wary crouch, holding the knife in front of him and slashing it back and forth through the frigid air.

"Steen, get up and help me, you miserable lump of coal," he called out to his accomplice.

"I'm hurt, Karl," the man named Steen whined from his place on the ground. "I think he broke my jaw."

"If you don't get up now," hissed Karl, "I'll break the rest of your bones."

"*Helfen Sie mir!*" shouted Sebastian in German, hoping that it was close enough to the Dutch to bring someone to his rescue.

Steen struggled to his feet, swooned for a moment and grabbed the wall for support. He reached under his jacket and pulled out a pistol. Sebastian's blood froze. He could not possibly miss at such short range, and he could not reach him to knock the pistol from his hand because Karl stood in the way with his flashing knife. Desperate thoughts ran through his mind. Could this be the end of his life? Was he to die here in a stinking alleyway like a trapped animal? What would become of his mother? What would become of Felipe?

The pistol fired, and Sebastian closed his eyes and flinched, waiting for the pain of the hot lead ball ripping through his bones, sinews and organs. But he felt no pain. He opened his eyes and saw that a tall man with a long black beard and wearing a dark suit had just struck Steen on the forearm with a heavy cane, causing the bullet to go astray.

While Sebastian stared momentarily at the new development, Karl grabbed the pouch. His knife flashed once through the air, severing the pouch from its strap. Karl turned and ran from the alleyway with Steen two steps behind him. Sebastian was left holding the pouchless strap in his hand and staring at the stranger who had just saved his life. The entire incident had taken less than two minutes. He picked up his hat and put it back on his head.

"Are you Sebastian Dominguez?" asked the stranger.

"Yes, I am."

"That's what I thought. I was just on my way to your home when I saw you from afar walking in the other direction. So I decided to follow you and speak to you while you were walking. Then suddenly you weren't there any more. I thought you must have stepped into a shop on the way so I went looking for you. I really didn't expect to find you fighting thugs in an alley, but I suppose it's a good thing that I did. Are you all right?"

Sebastian took stock of his limbs and his garments. No serious damage seemed to have been done.

"Yes," he said. "I think I'm all right. Except for my nerves, that is. It'll be a little while before they recover."

"It seems they got away with your pouch," said the stranger. "Was there anything important in it?"

"No, nothing at all. Some biscuits, some cheese and a piece of cracked lead pipe from our plumbing that I was supposed to drop off for repairs on the way to the bank. So you were coming to see me?"

"Yes, I was."

"Imagine that," said Sebastian. "This morning, Rabbi Aboab gives me a blessing that the Almighty should protect me from my enemies, and an hour later, a protector rescues me from my attackers. Amazing, isn't it?"

"If you say so."

"Why would you be looking for me?"

"My father wants to see you. He asked me to invite you

to his house."

"Might I ask you for your name?"

"You might. It's Amos."

"And your family name?"

"Strasbourg."

"Strasbourg! I can't believe it!"

"That's right. My name is Strasbourg. Amos Strasbourg. Is that so incredible?"

"No, it's not incredible. I mean, yes, it is incredible. I mean, I don't know what I mean. Why would someone named Strasbourg come looking for me today of all days? It's like a miracle."

"It's not much of a miracle, Dominguez."

"Call me Sebastian, and I'll call you Amos."

Amos shrugged. "Whatever pleases you. It's like this. You met with Rabbi Shlomo Strasbourg in Vienna, and you told him you were planning to settle in Amsterdam. My father, Rabbi Mordechai Strasbourg, is one of the rabbis of the Ashkenazi community here in Amsterdam. He and Rabbi Shlomo are first cousins. Their fathers were brothers. So Rabbi Shlomo wrote a letter to my father, telling him all about you and asking him to keep an eye on you. We heard last night that your family had come to Amsterdam, so my father asked me to call on you this morning. That's where I was going when you ran into a little trouble here. You can call this a miracle, but then I suppose everything that happens in this world can be called a miracle."

"All right. Let's just say it was good fortune."

"Whatever pleases you. I don't care. What did those thugs want from you? What were they expecting to find in the pouch?"

"It's a long story."

"If you've got the time, so do I. But if you don't want to tell me the story, that is also just fine. I just came to invite you to my father's house."

This time it was Sebastian's turn to shrug. "I don't mind telling you if we can talk while we walk. I'm on my way to the Bank of Amsterdam. Do I look presentable enough to meet with a banker?"

"Are you depositing money or withdrawing?" said Amos.

"Depositing."

"Then the banker's the one who has to worry about looking presentable, not you. You're the one with the money. You can dress any way you like."

"There is a certain logic to what you say," said Sebastian, "but I prefer to look somewhat presentable at all times."

"Portuguese dandy," said Amos, but there was a mischievous twinkle in his eye. "All right, I'll give you a straight answer. Your suit has smudges at the knees. Your shoes are scuffed. Your hat could use a brushing, and that orange feather is not going to tickle anyone's fancy ever again. That's about it. I would say you look presentable. Certainly presentable enough to meet a banker."

Sebastian could not help but laugh. "All right. You've made your point. Walk with me, and we'll talk."

The two men walked slowly through the cold sunlight. Sebastian told Amos about the ambush in the Black Forest and the attempt to steal his saddlebags. He told him how the dying Gunther had identified Karl as his leader and now a man named Karl had tried to steal his pouch.

"They probably thought your money was in your pouch," said Amos. "That's what they were after."

"Well, it wasn't in the pouch. It's in a special breast pocket I had sewn into this jacket."

"It's funny," said Amos. "Why didn't they kill you? They could have, you know. But they were only after the pouch. Real funny."

"That's not so funny," said Sebastian. "They could have

killed me back in the Black Forest too, but they didn't."

"So what were they after back then? Your safe passage from Sobieski? It had no value to them."

"But it had value to me. Maybe they didn't want me to have it."

"Hmm. Maybe. But why not just kill you?"

"What's with you, Amos? Do you mind if I live?"

Amos shrugged. "Whatever pleases you. But let's figure this out."

"Maybe they just want to hurt me," said Sebastian. "You know, steal my safe passage. Steal my money… Maybe whoever sent them doesn't have the stomach to kill me."

"And you don't think this same person or persons betrayed you to the authorities in Vienna and tried to get you shipped back to Spain? That's a pretty serious attempt to kill you."

"That's what Gonzalo said at the time. I didn't have an answer then, and I don't have one now. Would you like to come with me to the bank? When we're done I'll come with you to your father's house."

"Sounds fair."

When they arrived at the offices of the Bank of Amsterdam, Amos declined to come in to meet the banker with Sebastian. He had no desire to hear the private details of the Dominguez family's business. Instead, he chose to wait in one of the antechambers until Sebastian had concluded his business.

Sebastian was shown into a large counting room in which there were two ornate oak tables. A heavy man with a red face, red hair and an extravagant red mustache rose to greet him with his hand extended. A woman sat at the other table. She gave Sebastian a brief smile and busied herself with a pile of documents.

"*Goedemorgen en onthaal*," he said.

Sebastian stared at him. "Can we perhaps speak Portuguese or German?"

"Of course, Senhor Dominguez," he said, this time in Portuguese. "My apologies. I forgot that you are new here. Trust me, if you speak German, you will also be speaking Dutch in no time at all. The Ashkenazi Jews pick it up even faster because they speak Yiddish as well."

"I'm sure I will," said Sebastian.

The man rubbed his hands together. "So let me introduce myself. I am Johannes Hoogaboom, and this is my wife Wilhelmina. I am a director with the bank. My wife has no official standing at the bank, but she comes in to help me when things get very busy. You are probably not accustomed to seeing a woman in the counting room of a bank, but I assure you that Wilhelmina is as competent as any man, and more competent than most."

"I have no doubt that she is," said Sebastian. "Good day, senhora."

Wilhelmina Hoogaboom gave him the barest hint of a nod, but she did not speak.

"So what can we do for you, Senhor Dominguez?" said the director.

"I would like to open several accounts, some in my name, some in the names of others. Would that be all right?"

"Perfectly all right," said the director. "As long as you are putting money in and not taking it out. Heh heh."

"Heh heh," repeated Sebastian.

"How much will you be depositing?" asked the director.

"About one hundred and fifty thousand guilders."

The director's eyes bulged. "You have all this money with you? I would think you'd need a wagon to bring so much money. Heh heh."

"You would," said Sebastian. "But it's in the form of letters of credit. Much easier to carry around."

For the next hour, the paperwork for all the accounts was prepared and signed. The director explained all the intricacies of using the accounts to conduct business on the exchange.

"I want you to know, Senhor Dominguez," said the director, "that I rarely see such large sums of money being deposited at once by a single person, but I have seen it in the past. Yes, I have. And I have seen people lose it as well. If you lose it, do not say I haven't warned you. You will not be the first one to go bankrupt in this business. Bankruptcy is no disgrace for people doing business on the exchange. Just make sure it is an honest bankruptcy."

"What is an honest bankruptcy?" asked Sebastian.

"It means you made the wrong guess and the wrong investments, and you lost your money. Not you, Heaven forbid. You know what I mean. A dishonest bankruptcy is where you pull other people down with you even though they don't deserve to be pulled down. You will figure it out as you go along. If someone should do that, the authorities will punish him, and if he is Jewish, he will probably bring down the wrath of the Maamad on his head. Just be careful. Such large sums of money can be a temptation to overconfidence and recklessness."

"Thank you for the warning, Mijnheer Hoogaboom. I will be careful."

"Excellent, excellent." He stroked his mustache and gave Sebastian a speculative look. "Also, if you don't mind my asking, did something happen to you on the way here? There are marks on your garments. Maybe someone heard you were carrying a great sum of money and tried to relieve you of it. Eh?"

Sebastian smiled at the director. "You certainly have a vivid imagination for a bank official."

"Heh heh. That's what my wife always says. And speaking of my wife, she is a house agent. You will need a house, and since you can afford it, she can help you find one that is exactly to your liking. Do you want to hear what she has for you?"

"Why not?" said Sebastian. "I was going to look for a house once I had the accounts set up, so we might as well talk about it now."

"My dear wife," the director called out, "can you please set aside the documents for a little while and tell Senhor Dominguez what homes are available for him? He can pay a good price, but I want him to get full value for his money."

Wilhelmina Hoogaboom looked up from her documents and said, "I have something for you, something really nice, but it is fairly expensive. If you are only looking for a bargain, this is not the house for you. It has just come on the market, and it will not be on for very long."

"I'm listening," said Sebastian.

"The address is 12 Jodenbreestraat. That means the Jews' Broad Street. And it's right off the Houtgracht. Rembrandt — you know, the famous painter — used to live at 4 Jodenbreestraat, just down the street. If you'd come fifteen years earlier, you might have been neighbors, but he's dead now. The house is a large brick structure with four bedrooms, a brand-new kitchen, a stately dining room and salon, maid's quarters on the third floor and much more. It's been recently renovated and is in move-in condition. It is just two blocks from that beautiful Portuguese Synagogue you people built a few years ago. And it's right near the Etz Chaim school. If you're interested you'll have to make a bid on it right away. I'm not the only house agent offering it."

"How much do they want for it?" asked Sebastian.

"Four thousand seven hundred and fifty guilders."

"It sounds very good. Exactly what my mother would like. We'll look at it today. If she likes it, we can close the deal right away."

"Excellent. By the way, since the money is hot right now, I'd like to offer you a real bargain."

"I'm listening."

"I have a piece of land for sale. Two hundred acres."

Sebastian laughed. "You would need a king of a big country to buy such a large piece of land."

"It will cost you only one hundred and fifty guilders. Are you interested?"

"I don't understand. Where is this land? Under the sea?"

"Not quite, but not so far off. It is not under the sea. It is on the other side of the sea. Well, the ocean to be exact. It is in America. In a British colony called New Jersey. There's a large tract of land across the river from New Amsterdam. Well, it's not called New Amsterdam any more. They call it New York. This land is not developed. They call it the Meadowlands. It's a little swampy, but that's not so bad. You just have to drain it. People are investing in it these days. It's cheap, and the upside is good. Who knows what it will be worth some day? Some people think that the colonies have a big future, although I for one doubt it. But why not roll the dice with one hundred and fifty guilders?"

Sebastian thought for a moment. One hundred and fifty guilders? All things considered, it was a really paltry sum.

"Sure," he said. "Why not? I'll take it sight unseen. But the proof of ownership must be in perfect order. According to what I've heard, some people will sell the same piece of land over and over again to many different buyers."

"Senhor Dominguez! I would never do such a thing!"

"I didn't mean that you would do it. Perish the thought. I meant that the people offering it to you might be unscrupulous."

"I am an experienced and respectable house agent, Senhor Dominguez. You need have no worries. Do we have a deal?"

"Yes, we do."

"Then by tomorrow at this time, you may be a landowner on both sides of the Atlantic Ocean."

# THE SEEDS
## OF FRIENDSHIP · 5

F ELIPE'S BREATH CAME IN FROSTY CLOUDS as he stood
motionless outside the squat building on the
Uilenburgerstraat, unable to work up the courage to go any
further. His thoughts were in turmoil. He knew that he
should and would do as Rabbi Aboab had instructed him,
but for the moment, he was immobilized, unable to go forward or turn back.

One of the windows on the second floor was slightly
open, and he could hear the sweet, innocent sounds of young
children singing the words of the Chumash with the joy and
excitement of discovery. In his mind, he pictured the classrooms in which the older boys studied with their rabbis.

The sounds in those rooms would be different. There
would be arguments and discussions and heated debates,
and all of it would resonate with a more sophisticated joy
derived from the satisfaction of intense intellectual exploration blended with the spiritual fulfillment of probing divine
knowledge. And yet, there was a commonality between the
joy of the little children and the joy of the advanced students.
Both emanated came from the deepest wellsprings of the soul
in touch with its Creator.

*This*, thought Felipe, *is where I belong*. He took a deep
breath and opened the door. As he stepped into the building,

he felt he had crossed an important threshold and was stepping into his future.

There was no one in the hallway when he came in, and he spent a few minutes wandering about on his own, stopping beside different classrooms and listening for a while before he moved on.

"Wonderful, isn't it?" said a voice behind him.

Felipe turned and saw a young man holding a sheaf of papers.

"*Shalom aleichem*," the young man said, and he extended his hand. "Welcome to Yeshivat Etz Chaim. My name is Obadiah Abendana. I am one of the teachers here, among my other duties. And you are?"

Felipe shook the proffered hand. "I'm pleased to meet you. My name is Felipe Dominguez."

"Ah, yes. We have heard that your family was arriving in Amsterdam. A double welcome to you then. Is there anything I can do for you? Anything in particular that you need?"

"Rabbi Aboab sent me here," said Felipe. "He said I should speak with Rabbi Sasportas."

"Aha! I'm beginning to understand. Did Rabbi Aboab also say that Rabbi Sasportas should give you breakfast?"

"Indeed, he did."

"Whenever he sends over a prospective student, Rabbi Aboab sends along a message about breakfast. I perform this duty on behalf of Rabbi Sasportas. Come, I will give you breakfast, and then we will go meet the rabbi."

Obadiah prepared a spread of pita, olives, cheese and tea in a windowless cubicle off the kitchen.

"I just ate a half hour ago," Obadiah said. "But you must be hungry. I'll have some tea and keep you company."

"If you're not eating," said Felipe, "can you tell me something about the rabbi, I mean, what to expect?"

"Of course. Do you know anything about him?"

Felipe shook his head. "I've never heard of him."

"Well, most people have. He is world famous."

"As a scholar?"

"Partially. But more so because of an unpopular position he took about twenty years ago. You go ahead and eat. I'll tell you the whole story. You see, Rabbi Aboab is very much one of us, a Marrano born in Portugal, but Rabbi Sasportas is from Oran in Algeria. Neither he nor his family ever went through the Marrano experience. He was brought up in the ways of the Torah from the moment he came into this world. By the time he was twenty-four years old, he was already such an accomplished scholar that he was invited to become the rabbi of Tiemçen in Algeria. Later he was rabbi in Morocco in the important cities of Fez and afterward in Salé. Then he was in prison for a while about thirty years ago, but he escaped and came to Amsterdam with his family."

"Why was he in prison?" asked Felipe.

"It was something political, but I don't know the details."

"Did you ever ask the rabbi about it?"

Obadiah laughed. "The rabbi is a little frightening. You don't just chat with him about his past. I think it had something to do with a rebellion in Morocco, but I'm really not clear about any of it. Anyway, as I was saying, the rabbi came to Amsterdam where he found refuge for a few years. He got to know us and we got to know him, and the next thing there was a real rapport. Then he became the rabbi of the Portuguese community in London established by Rabbi Menasheh ben Israel, and when there was an outbreak of plague, he left London and became the rabbi of the Portuguese community in Hamburg. That brings us to 1666. And you know what happened in that year, don't you?"

"I was only six years old at the time," said Felipe. "Are you talking about Shabbetai Tzvi, the false Messiah? I never heard about it back in Spain, but I heard the whole story in Metz. Quite an episode, wasn't it?"

"Yes, it was. He had just about everyone convinced that he was the Messiah come at last to redeem the Jewish people and bring an end to our long and dark exile. Only a few rabbis dared raise their voices against him. You see, the Cossacks had just killed a half million Jews in Poland and the Ukraine, and the people were desperate for a ray of hope. They could not bear to continue living in exile, being persecuted and always under the threat of massacre. They wanted the Messiah, and they wanted him right away. And the Portuguese communities, they had their own special reasons for supporting that impostor. Many people coming out of a Marrano life in Spain and Portugal felt religiously inferior to other Jews. The Messiah would make all Jews equal, and that really appealed to them."

"So let me take a guess," said Felipe. "Rabbi Sasportas was one of the rabbis who spoke out against Shabbetai Tzvi."

"Good guess. But it was not so simple. The Portuguese community of Hamburg was wild in its support for Shabbetai Tzvi. People were selling their houses and packing their bags. People were dancing in the streets. It was mass euphoria and mass hysteria. And in that environment, Rabbi Sasportas shouted his condemnations from the pulpit and wrote sizzling letters to Eretz Yisrael and communities all over Europe. Can you imagine what it was like for him in Hamburg? Can you imagine the pressures he was under from his own people?"

"I imagine they were very intense."

"Intense isn't the word for it. It was like a rumbling volcano. Most rabbis would have crumbled under the pressure, but not Rabbi Sasportas. He stood up for his beliefs with no thought about what would happen to him personally. Would they remove him from his position? Would they take away his house and his income? Would they humiliate him in the streets? None of these things mattered. Only the truth and the honor of the Almighty. He was a ferocious lion, a fearless champion of truth. He was thunder and lightning, and he let nothing stand in his way. It was his voice — and a few other voices like his — that prevented the impostor from gaining a total victory. And when it was all over, when the impostor was finally exposed as the fraud that he was, the entire Jewish people looked at Rabbi Sasportas with respect and admiration."

"Amazing," said Felipe. "So when and why did he leave Hamburg?"

"I think it was in 1673. He was invited to become *rosh midrash* of one of the smaller *yeshivot* here in Amsterdam. He was here for a couple of years, and then he became *rosh midrash* in Livorno in Italy. Then he came back four years ago to become *rosh midrash* in Etz Chaim, the main yeshivah of Amsterdam. I guess he discovered he likes running a yeshivah better than being a congregation rabbi."

"I can understand that. So when do I get to meet him?"

"Right now," said Obadiah. "Unless you want something else to eat. You've hardly taken a bite."

"I'm too nervous to eat. Let's go."

The rabbi's room was on the first floor, tucked away in a quiet corner where he would not be disturbed by the raucous shouts of exuberant young boys. Obadiah knocked lightly on the door. He waited until he heard the sound of a tinkling bell, and then he opened the door. The rabbi was sitting with his back to a large window through which bright sunlight streamed. A large Gemara was open in front of him on a mahogany table with ornately carved legs. A tiny bell sat on the table next to the Gemara.

The rabbi looked at Felipe and nodded in greeting. "*Shalom aleichem*," he said in a barely audible voice. He did not extend his hand.

"This is Felipe Dominguez," said Obadiah.

The rabbi arched his eyebrows, signaling that he recognized the name.

"Rabbi Aboab sent him to the rabbi," continued Obadiah. "He wants the rabbi to take him under his wing."

The rabbi raised one eyebrow, signaling a question.

Obadiah nodded. "Yes," he said. "I have already served him breakfast."

The rabbi looked directly at Obadiah and nodded twice. Obadiah bowed slightly, backed out of the room and closed the door behind him.

The rabbi turned his head slightly, raising his eyebrows and pointing his nose toward a chair that stood on the right side of the table. Felipe edged over to the chair and sat down, hoping he had read the signal correctly.

"You want to learn here?" he said in a voice that was barely above a whisper.

"Yes," said Felipe. "More than anything else."

The rabbi nodded. "I am nearly seventy-five years old, and in my old age, I find that talking takes an effort. I try to save my talking strength for the Torah. Do you have a Hebrew name?"

"Yes. It is Pinhas. My name is Pinhas Dominguez."

"When did you learn to read Hebrew?"

"Four years ago. When we left Spain."

"How long have you been studying Torah?"

"Almost the entire four years."

"How long have you been studying Gemara?"

"Maybe three and a half years."

"Good. Tell me what you know."

On the other side of the island of Vlooyenburg, alongside the Herrengracht, Sebastian and Amos were passing through a Jewish neighborhood Sebastian had not yet seen. Despite the cold, the streets were teeming with people shopping, carrying packages or just plain arguing with each other. Peddlers hawked bolts of cloth, trinkets and all sorts of other merchandise from pushcarts. Some of them had fires going in braziers to warm themselves and to attract customers. Unlike the Portuguese, the men did not wear colorful suits or feathered hats, and they grew their beards long for the most part. Sebastian recognized the language spoken in these streets as Yiddish because of its resemblance to German, but he barely understood a word of what the people were saying.

"We turn here," said Amos. He pointed to a narrow two-story house. "That house, that's where we live."

"You live with your parents?" asked Sebastian.

Amos's shoulders twitched almost imperceptibly. "I have two small rooms at the back of the house. I have my own door to the street. My parents have their privacy."

Sebastian realized he had unwittingly touched a raw nerve. During their walk back from the bank, he felt he had gotten to know this odd man named Amos Strasbourg to a certain extent, and he decided that he liked him. The two men were close in age, although Amos was probably two or three years older. His cynical remarks and comments were generally amusing and never malicious or spiteful. They seemed to be derived from a fatalistic attitude toward life and a tragic sadness that was never far from the surface. Sebastian guessed that Amos had somehow been hurt badly and that he carried his burden of pain with him wherever he went. *Apparently*, Sebastian thought, *his living in the same house as his parents had something to do with it. But maybe not.* He didn't know Amos well enough to make an accurate guess.

A jolly woman with a round face, an apron and a large white cap opened the door. "No, I am not the maid," she said when she saw Sebastian's shaven face and orange ostrich feather. "I am Yocheved Strasbourg, and you must be Sebastian Dominguez."

"At your service, senhora."

She clapped her hands with delight. "Oh, I just love Portuguese. All those *zh*'s and *ao*'s. Such a pretty language. Of course, I just love Yiddish, too. It is such a rich language, so full of Jewish experiences and feelings. But I'm such a silly woman. Why am I keeping you standing here on the doorstep? My husband is waiting eagerly for you. Come in. Come in. *Boa vinda a nossa casa.*" She stopped and cocked her head. "Did you understand that?"

"Of course, senhora," said Sebastian. "You welcomed me to your house."

"That I did. And in Portuguese! Oh, I'm so proud of myself. I never thought you'd understand my Portuguese with such a heavy Yiddish accent."

"Oh no, senhora. Your Portuguese is excellent."

"You are very kind. But you've just heard all of it. Maybe I'll learn a few more words if you visit us here once in a while. Come this way. You can sit in the dining room. I'll let my husband know that you're here."

"Mother can be a little outrageous," Amos murmured to Sebastian, "but she is a thoroughly good person."

"Yes, I can see that," said Sebastian.

The door was flung open, and a tall man with a long gray beard rushed into the room as if he was running to catch a boat pulling away from the shore. His waistcoat was completely open, and his *tzitzis* flapped. His eyes swung back and forth and settled on Sebastian. A green and yellow parrot sat on his shoulder.

He grabbed Sebastian's hand in both of his hands and shook it up and down, up and down a number of times before he released it.

"Sebastian Dominguez!" he cried. "What an honor! What an honor!"

"The honor is all mine," said Sebastian.

Rabbi Strasbourg flung up his hand and waved the remark aside. "You're just being a gentleman. Do you mind if I call you Sebastian?"

Sebastian shook his head.

"I mean, I'm old enough to be your father. I would say you're about the same age as Amos, maybe a little younger. So! I'm so glad you came. Amos didn't have to force you, did he? I'm just joking. Everyone knows that Mordechai Strasbourg likes to make jokes. But I'll have you know that Mordechai Strasbourg also has a serious side, and one of these days I'm gong to find it."

Amos gave his father an indulgent smile. "Be careful, Sebastian," he said. "There is a very sharp mind behind the humorous façade."

The door opened and Rebbetzin Strasbourg came in with a tray of refreshments.

"Façade?" she said. "Did someone say something about the façade? We had it painted before the summer. Did you say something good or something bad?"

"We were not talking about the house, Mother," said Amos.

"Oh," she said. "Never mind. I'll leave you men to your serious discussions. I have work to do in the kitchen. Do you want me to take the parrot, Rabbi?"

"You want to take Hurdus?" said her husband. "Why? He won't bother us. I'll just give him one of these crackers."

The rebbetzin went off to the kitchen, and the man sat down at the table.

"What does the bird's name mean?" asked Sebastian.

"First of all, let me teach you something. You don't call a parrot a bird, at least not in this house. A crow is a bird. A sparrow is a bird. A pigeon is a bird. Even an eagle is a bird. But a parrot is not a bird. It's a parrot. And his name? It's Hurdus. Hurdus — some call him Herod — was an evil king of the Jews about two thousand years ago. I imagine they didn't let his soul into Heaven so he had to find someplace to be. Something tells me he chose my parrot. Who knows? Living in a good Jewish home for fifteen years may be just what he needs to get them to let him into Heaven."

Sebastian smiled and nodded. "I see."

"No, you don't. You're just being a gentleman again. But I don't mind." His voice changed subtly, and his face grew somewhat more serious. "My cousin Rabbi Shlomo Strasbourg wrote to me about you. Someone is stalking you, and that is no laughing matter."

"It is more serious than you think," said Amos, and he went on to tell Rabbi Strasbourg about everything that had happened that morning and about the ambush in the Black Forest.

The rabbi grew very grave. "Do you have any ideas about this, Sebastian? Who could be stalking you? And why?"

"I'm afraid not, Rabbi Strasbourg," said Sebastian. "And the most puzzling thing is that this stalker cannot seem to make up his mind if he wants to kill me or not. He could have had me killed in the Black Forest and this morning as well, but he didn't. Yet he betrayed me to the authorities in Vienna and almost had me shipped back to Spain where I most likely would not have survived for very long. I'm wondering if there may be two different stalkers."

Rabbi Strasbourg shook his head. "It is more reasonable to assume that there is only one. But what does he want? Who would gain by your death, Sebastian?"

"No one. Except for my family, that is."

"You mean your immediate family?"

"Yes. My mother, brother and sister."

"Well, I think we can count them out," said the rabbi. "Do you have more distant relatives?"

"Not that I'm aware of. At least, not Jewish ones. I may have some Marrano cousins back in Spain, but I wouldn't know about them. We pretty much kept to ourselves. Our family was almost entirely from the Spanish nobility."

"I'm aware of that. So we know of no relatives. Who else would benefit?"

"I don't know."

"Maybe it's someone close to you. It could be, you know. Sometimes it's the person you least suspect."

"I have very few people close to me," said Sebastian. "I wish we could have caught that Karl and his friend Steen today."

"What would you have done," said the rabbi, "if you'd caught them?"

"Off with their heads!" shouted a hoarse voice. "Throw them to the dogs!"

The rabbi turned his head to face the parrot perched on his shoulder. "Behave yourself, Hurdus," he said. "If you don't get your violent impulses under control, you'll never get into Heaven. Here, have another cracker."

Sebastian chuckled. "It's not funny, but it's funny. I'm inclined to agree with Hurdus. I would have wanted to chop off their heads, but not until they had told me who was behind these attacks."

"So I think the next step should be to try and find them," said the rabbi. "They followed you to Vienna. They followed you back from Vienna. They probably stalked you in France. And now they're stalking you in Amsterdam. I'm assuming they haven't gone back to Bavaria or Swabia or whichever German-speaking corner of Europe they're from. No, I'm assuming that they're still right here in Amsterdam. We have to find them."

"But how?"

"We know their names, at least their first names. We have their descriptions. We have the scar on Karl's bald head. I would say those are pretty good starting points. Amos, what do you think about getting Netzach involved?"

"What is *netzach*?" said Sebastian.

"He's a young man named Netzach Tomashov. Another of my cousin Shlomo's people. Without getting into details, the young man had a rough childhood, but Amsterdam is a good place for making a new start. Just about everyone here has come to start over again, in one way or another, for one reason or another. Netzach and his wife Kreindel live in that nice house next door with their two little twin girls, Chavah and Chanah. He makes a good living as a carpenter, and he has many contacts among the Dutch laborers. Maybe he can help us find this Karl and Steen. What do you think, Amos?"

He cocked his head. "It could be. Should I go look for him? He may have come home for lunch."

"Yes," said the rabbi. "Please do."

Amos stood up. "I'll be right back."

The rabbi waited until the door had closed before he spoke again.

"I'm happy for this opportunity to speak with you alone, Sebastian," he said. "Except for Hurdus here, of course. Amos likes you. I can see that. He doesn't take a liking to most people, but I think he has taken a liking to you. Amos needs a friend. If you would befriend him, I would be forever grateful."

Sebastian squirmed a little, unsure of where this was going. "Amos has my friendship already. He saved my life this morning. I mean, maybe he saved my life this morning. We're not sure about the intentions of those thugs. But he certainly saved me from injury or worse."

"I mean real friendship, Sebastian, not gratitude. Let me tell you something about Amos. My wife and I have three other children, all married. One lives in London. The other two in Krakow. Amos was also married. After his wedding, he moved to Hamburg, where his father-in-law took him into his importing business. We heard that they were expecting a child, and the next thing we heard was that his wife had died in childbirth."

"I am so sorry to hear that. And the child?"

"The child did not survive either."

"What a tragedy."

"Yes, a terrible tragedy. Some people can deal with this type of tragedy, but Amos was shattered. He used to be full of life and joy, but now, he is ... I don't know ... I was going to say bitter, but I don't think that's the right word. Bitter, at least, would be a strong feeling. I'd say he's more ... resigned ... detached ... as if he's disconnected himself from life. Do you know what I mean?"

"I think so."

"Amos came back here to Amsterdam to heal his wounds. He wanted to find his own place, but we insisted that he live with us. We felt he needed our love and support. We compromised by giving him his own quarters with his own entrance. The only way into our house from his apartment is through the street."

"I understand," said Sebastian, recalling Amos' earlier reaction.

"Amos has been home for nearly a year," said the rabbi, "and he has still not recovered. Sometimes, I think his hurt is so deep that he will never recover. But I have faith in the Almighty, the Healer of souls and broken hearts. And I think that maybe He has sent you to bring him back to life. I think that — " He stopped and cupped his and behind his ear. "They're coming. I hear them. Of course, I don't have to tell you not to say a word to Amos about our conversation."

The door opened, and Amos came, in followed by a husky young man in his late twenties.

"Off with their heads!" shouted Hurdus. "Throw them to the dogs!"

"Enough already, Hurdus," said the rabbi. "It's funny the first time, and then it becomes annoying. Think of a different line."

# A HURRICANE IN JAMAICA · 6

W INTER PASSED, AND SPRING CAME SOFTLY to Amsterdam. The Dominguez family settled comfortably into the new life. The betrayals, persecutions and assaults of the previous year came to an end, and after a while, everything seemed to have taken place in a bad dream, a dream from which they had thankfully awoken.

The house on the Jodenbreestraat turned out to be even better than the agent had said it was. Although a far cry from the Dominguez mansion in Spain, it was a vast improvement over their modest lodgings in Paris and Metz. The rooms were spacious, well appointed with rich mahogany moldings and completely furnished in a style that suited Doña Angelica's impeccable taste. Sebastian and Felipe each had the privacy of his own bedroom. And there was also a guest bedroom for when Carolina and Uriel would come to visit. In addition, there were two decent-sized bedrooms on the third floor, as well as a maid's room for Helga the Norwegian.

Doña Angelica was happier than she had been in a long time. She was welcomed easily into the highest circles of Portuguese society. She had no financial concerns. She was not a profligate spender, and she found she could spend within reason without worrying about the costs. She occupied her time by joining different benevolent societies. She visited the sick, and she raised money for the local charities. She spent a lot of time deflecting matches people suggested for the thirty-one-year-old Sebastian and the twenty-four-year-old Felipe, two of the most eligible bachelors in the Portuguese community of Amsterdam, where men did not usually marry until they were well into their twenties. She explained that her sons needed a few months to establish themselves, each in his own way, before either one would think of marriage.

Marriage was certainly not on Felipe's mind during his first few months in Amsterdam. Rabbi Sasportas had taken a real liking to him, and the two of them spent many hours each day studying together. It took a few weeks before Felipe could muster up the courage to argue and defend his point of view against the venerable rabbi without reservation, but once he reached that comfort zone, his progress was rapid. The old rabbi was impressed with his new disciple's sharp mind, invigorated by the energy of youth and the drive of an ambitious scholar, and he often found himself deferring to the young man's arguments.

One day, Rabbi Sasportas saw that Felipe had a disturbed look on his face that he quickly concealed when he saw that he was being observed.

"What is the matter, Pinhas?" said the old rabbi.

"It is nothing."

"It is not nothing. Perhaps you don't want to talk, but it is not nothing."

Felipe sighed. "I am concerned about myself and my family. I am wondering if we are really Jewish."

The old rabbi lifted his eyebrows. "Explain."

"We have been living as Christians for hundreds of years, violating the laws of the Torah practically every day. Does this still qualify us as Jews? Or do we need to convert if we want to be authentic Jews?"

The rabbi patted Felipe's cheek and saw that his hand came away moist. "You touch on a good point. There was a big dispute among the rabbis over two hundred years ago about the status of the Marranos. The problem was exactly as you say. The Marranos, for the most part, had the option of leaving and living as Jews elsewhere. Some rabbis called them *avarianim*, sinners, and insisted that they needed conversion like any other gentile coming to convert, at least the later generations did. Other rabbis called them *anusim*, people forced to sin, and considered them still authentic Jews. In our community, we say that someone descended from sincere *conversos*, genuine converts to Christianity, needs to be converted. But if the family lived as secret Jews, even for generations, we consider them authentic Jews, and we do not require conversion."

Felipe was relieved, but he still had a doubtful look on his face.

"Pinhas, my dear son," said the old rabbi, "if I had a young and beautiful daughter I'd give you her hand in marriage without a second thought. You're as Jewish as I am. And a lot more clever. But you're catching me in my old age. You'd never win so many arguments with me if I were fifty years younger!"

Felipe felt a burden lift from his heart. Over lunch that afternoon, he told Doña Angelica and Sebastian about his conversation with Rabbi Sasportas. His mother and brother had not been troubled by the same misgivings. It had never occurred to them, after all the sacrifices they had made, that they might not even be authentic Jews. It was only Felipe's scholarly mind that had raised the issue, and they were all relieved that Rabbi Sasportas had laid it to rest.

"I just have one question," said Doña Angelica. "Rabbi Sasportas may not have an eligible daughter, but does he have any granddaughters? And if not for you, maybe for your older brother. I repeat, older."

Sebastian laughed, but he did not respond. He excused

himself and went off to an appointment with one of the traders on the Exchange.

Sebastian's first months in Amsterdam were good ones. The accounts had been set up securely, the funds had been disbursed, the properties had been purchased and the investment account with the Exchange had been established. He bought Gonzalo a tavern in a gentile neighborhood not more than a twelve-minute walk from the house on the Jodenbreestraat, and he visited him from time to time. He also entrusted Gonzalo with a nest egg of three thousand guilders for safekeeping. "Do not give it to me," Sebastian told him, "unless everything has absolutely fallen apart. Do not give it to me if I need it for business, no matter how much I plead with you. This is emergency money."

Sebastian's first tentative steps on the Exchange were conservative. He made a modest investment in sugar futures and sold off his shares when they rose moderately. Although sugar prices rose very high afterward, he was more than content with the respectable profit he had earned. He did not enjoy the game of risk, nor did he have the pressures of immediate financial need. Low risk and low reward were perfectly acceptable to him. After the sugar trade, he ventured into wheat, spices, timber, whiskey and other commodities. Most of the time, he made a profit. Only once did he take a loss, and it was a relatively minor one. As time went on, he gained confidence in his trading abilities and his understanding of the markets. He still remained conservative, but he broadened his scope and increased the number of his investments.

His friendship with Amos was also growing and deepening. Amos had an importing business, and he occasionally traded on the Exchange, especially when he gained some valuable information through his business contacts. The two friends had a tacit agreement, however, to keep business and friendship separate. Nonetheless, they often discussed the economy in general and various things that were happening in Amsterdam and on the Exchange.

As he spent more time in the markets and in the company of Amos, and as Felipe spent more time in the *beis midrash*, the closeness between the two brothers diminished. Of course, they still loved each other as much as ever, but they no longer had so many common interests.

Sebastian loved the prayers, and he attended the rabbi's classes on Chumash, especially enjoying the discussions of moral and ethical issues that the rabbi's remarks usually sparked. He also attended classes on Halachah with great interest; after all, he wanted and needed to know how to conduct himself.

But he did not find the intricacy of Talmud study as exciting as Felipe did. In fact, he found that more than anything else, it confused him. On more than one occasion, he watched Felipe deep in a heated argument over a piece of Gemara or a passage in one of Rambam's works, and he felt a stab of envy. He knew that the ultimate goal of Torah study was to master the Talmud and the other ancient expositions of the inner workings of Torah Sheb'al'peh, the Oral Law, because these were the basis of Halachah and all Jewish thought. But his mind could not get past the surface of the texts.

Felipe insisted his problem was his unfamiliarity with the language, but Sebastian knew that it was more than that. He believed that if he tried really hard, he could get somewhere, but he knew he would never achieve the brilliant mastery Felipe was manifesting more and more each day.

In the early summer, news arrived in Amsterdam about a devastating hurricane in the British colony of Jamaica in the Caribbean Sea. Jamaica was a major producer of sugar, and the hurricane was sure to have a tremendous effect on the price of sugar. The more of the crop that was laid waste, the less sugar there would be for the world market, and the higher the price would climb.

The Exchange was a brick structure shaped as an enormous rectangle with its center, like a completely enclosed inner courtyard, open to the sky. Most of the trading activity took place in the covered porticos on all four sides of the open areas. Generally, the trading activities for different commodities were centered in different parts of the Exchange, the more prestigious under the overhangs of the porticos, protected from the rains, and the less important ones in the open area in the middle.

By eleven-thirty on the morning after the news about Jamaica arrived, the streets around the Exchange were thronged with hundreds of traders just waiting in the scorching heat to get in on the trading as soon as the doors opened at noon.

Amos and Sebastian were among the early arrivals, and they had a position near the door.

"Are you holding any sugar futures?" asked Amos.

"No, I try not to speculate," said Sebastian. "I don't gamble at cards, and I don't gamble with commodities."

"That's a good policy. If I'd followed such a policy over the years, I would have a lot more money than I do now. Unlike you, I do have some sugar futures. I bought sugar for delivery next week at last week's price. The trader who sold it to me thought the price would go down, but it looks like the price is going to skyrocket, and I'm going to make a handsome profit."

"Good for you," said Sebastian. "Right now, I'm holding a small block of sugar shares. I've already paid for them, so it's an investment, not speculation. If, or rather when, the price goes up, I'll sell my shares and make some profit, too."

"Here we go," said Amos, as the doors were flung open and the crowd of eager traders pressed forward. "Hey, don't push!"

As the crowd poured onto the trading floor, all other commodities were forgotten. It was all about sugar, and only sugar. Everyone knew the price was about to skyrocket, but it would take a while until it reached its peak. There was profit to be made by buying early, even at an inflated price, and selling out when the price climbed really high.

"Sugar shares for sixty," shouted one trader.

"Done," shouted a buyer.

"Sixty-six," shouted another seller.

"Done."

This went on and on until the prices had climbed to eighty-nine, and there seemed no end in sight. The shouting grew so loud that it was impossible to hear anything at a normal decibel level.

Amos grabbed Sebastian by the collar and shouted into his ear. "Come on, this is a great opportunity. The price is going to pass two hundred easily. We can still buy for under a hundred and double our money."

Sebastian hesitated. This could not really be called speculation. What were the risks? Where was the gamble? Even a moderate hurricane would ravage the sugar plantations to such a degree that prices would shoot up. And this was reported as a devastating hurricane. A worldwide shortage was inevitable. Within a few hours, the small window of opportunity would be closed, but right now, there was an easy profit to be made.

"Don't do it," shouted a voice at his shoulder.

Sebastian turned and saw a man in the garb of a Portuguese trader. He had a trimmed red beard that came to a sharp point beneath his chin and kindly blue eyes. Sebastian had seen him often in the synagogue, but they had a nodding acquaintance at most. Sebastian had never spoken a word to him. He did not even know the man's name.

"Why not?" he shouted back across the mad din.

"It's a lie."

"What did you say?" said Amos.

"I said it's a lie," said the man.

Amos and Sebastian exchanged glances. Amos shook his head and signaled to Sebastian and the man to follow him outside.

"What are you saying?" said Amos as soon as they reached the relative serenity of the busy street.

"I'm saying that it's a lie," said the man.

"That's what I thought you said," said Amos. "I don't know if you're telling the truth or not. But there's no point in taking a chance, is there?"

"My friend is a little upset," said Sebastian. "He thought he was about to make a very handsome profit, and you burst his bubble."

"I didn't cause him a loss," said the man. "I prevented him from taking a loss. There was no hurricane in Jamaica."

"Listen, I know you, sort of," said Sebastian, "but I don't know your name. My name is Sebastian Dominguez."

"I know your name," said the man. "You're famous. Everyone knows who you are and all about your history. My name is Diego Zuzarte, and I'm not famous. But I do know certain things. And I know that there was no hurricane in Jamaica."

"How do you know?" said Amos, a little less belligerently this time.

"Because I have close connections," said Zuzarte, "with the sea captains who sail to the West Indies. And with plenty of sea captains who sail to the East Indies and other ports in Asia. I was down at the docks this morning checking out the rumor of the hurricane. None of them heard about it. They laughed it off."

"So someone started the rumor to drive up the price," said Sebastian. "Then once it gets really high he sells off and leaves the buyer holding the sugar when the price collapses."

"That's right," said Zuzarte. "The buyer could have been the two of you."

Amos reached for Zuzarte's hand and shook it. "I believe you. Your words have the ring of truth. Thank you very much for saving us from a possible disaster. I understand you couldn't very well have announced it in there. No one would have believed you. They probably would have trampled you or tossed you out. But why did you decide to tell us, of all people?"

"It wasn't because of you, my friend," said Zuzarte.

"Why?" said Amos. "Because I'm a Tudesco?"

Tudesco was the Portuguese word for a German Jew and was applied to all Ashkenazi Jews. After the horrendous massacres in Poland and the persecutions in the other countries of eastern and central Europe, thousands of Jews had fled to what they considered safer places. Amsterdam had been one of the destinations of choice because of its reputation for religious freedom and economic opportunity. The number of Ashkenazi Jews soon surpassed the number of Portuguese Jews, and tensions arose between the two communities.

"I don't have anything against Tudescos, my friend," said Zuzarte. "But why would I choose to tell you of all people, if I don't even know your name?"

"Good point," conceded Amos. "So it was because of Sebastian here. Even though he didn't know your name."

"Good point," conceded Zuzarte with a friendly twinkle in his eyes. "But it's not as if Dominguez and I don't know each other at all, you know. We see each other in the synagogue every Shabbat, and we nod to each other and murmur our Shabbat Shaloms. So when I overheard him consider taking the plunge into sugar, I warned him. You were lucky to be standing there at the same time. You could have taken a big loss, you know."

"Yes, I know," said Amos. "Thank you. I wonder who started this rumor."

"It probably wasn't one person," said Zuzarte. "I have experience with these things, you know. I've seen it happen a number of times before. A group gets together and plans to manipulate the market by starting rumors. They buy up shares of sugar, for instance, or whatever else has caught their interest, at a low price. Then they start rumors of shortages, driving up the price. Then they sell out at a profit. Then people discover that the rumor is false. Then the price collapses. Then the poor unsuspecting buyers take a big loss."

"What an evil thing to do," said Sebastian. "And all in the name of business. I hope no one of the Jewish community, Portuguese or Tudesco, was involved."

"Pipe dreams," said Zuzarte with a rueful smile. "Unfortunately, Jews are capable of some pretty awful things if they're driven by greed or other strong desires. Anyway, come, let me buy you gentlemen something to eat."

A deafening rumble of noise erupted from the Exchange behind them. The three men ran back inside. A Portuguese Jew in a green suit and a Tudesco in a long black coat were swinging at each other, and soon, they were locked in a clinch, scuffling and rolling on the ground, pummeling each other but doing little damage. A crowd of traders was gathered around them, shouting encouragement to one or the other or sometimes both.

In the background, a trader shouted, "Sugar at sixty-one. Who wants sugar at sixty-one?"

There were no takers.

"Fifty-nine?" shouted the trader.

Still no takers.

Sebastian caught sight of Eduardo Colon, the *parnas* who had come to welcome them to Amsterdam. Colon was an active trader, and Sebastian had seen him often at the

Exchange. This day, he was wearing a yellow suit with blue trim.

"What's happening here, senhor?" he asked.

"You missed the excitement, senhor Dominguez," said Colon. "The rumor about the hurricane in Jamaica was exposed as false, and the price of sugar instantly collapsed. That Tudesco there made an offer at one hundred and thirty-three right before the price collapsed. Then he took back his offer. He claimed he never made an offer. He was only considering it. So they started calling each other names and fighting. It's highly improper."

"What's going to happen?"

"Well, the Tudesco is going to have to pay. His offer was recorded and registered, and there's nothing he can do about it. If he doesn't pay, he'll be barred from the Exchange and dragged into court. And the two of them will probably be fined for their disgraceful behavior."

The closing bell rang.

"Ah, it's two o'clock," said Colon. "It's a good thing the Exchange is only open for two hours a day. Imagine what kind of trouble there would be if it were open longer. People have to learn how to behave properly. Well, I shall be going. Good day."

Colon turned and walked away, his head held high, his yellow back fading slowly through the crowd until it completely disappeared.

# OFFERS OF MATRIMONY · 7

T WO WEEKS LATER, FELIPE WAS ENGAGED to be married to Rebecca Pinto, the daughter of Emanuel and Sarah Pinto. Senhor Pinto, originally of Rotterdam, was a noted financier with family connections to the fabulously wealthy Pinto brothers. It all happened very quickly. One day, Senhor Pinto visited Rabbi Sasportas and mentioned that he was looking for a son-in-law of sterling character and brilliance in Torah, a young man who could one day head the yeshivah he was establishing in the Hague. Rabbi Sasportas immediately suggested Pinhas Dominguez, his favorite disciple.

Doña Angelica was intrigued by the match, especially because the suggestion had come from Rabbi Sasportas, who loved Felipe like a son. She arranged to meet with the girl first and found her lovely and charming. Felipe and Rebecca met several times over the next few days. Then her parents met with Doña Angelica to discuss practical matters. Rabbi Sasportas made sure that everything went very smoothly, and the match was finalized.

The Pintos threw a lavish party in their home on the St. Antoniesbreestraat, not far from the mansions of his cousins, the famous Pinto brothers. Most of the prominent people of the Amsterdam community, Portuguese and Tudesco, came to congratulate the bride and groom and their families, but there were more colorful suits and plumed hats than black hats and coats among the men.

Eduardo Colon outdid himself in a lavender suit trimmed in midnight blue with a white lace collar and cuffs. His hat was adorned by a cluster of ostrich feathers in an assortment of colors. He circulated among the guests with a glass of wine in his hand, offering comments and accepting compliments, with Martino Vega, his colleague on the Maamad, trailing along beside him.

After Colon finished paying his respects to the Pinto family, immediate and extended, he sought out Doña Angelica and offered her his most heartfelt congratulations.

"Senhora Dominguez, this is a wonderful day," he said, "for your family, for the Pinto family — I hear that your son is a brilliant young scholar — and for all of Amsterdam. It is a day of rejoicing."

"Thank you so much, Senhor Colon," she replied, genuinely pleased.

"And may I offer my congratulations as well," said Martino Vega.

"Oh, thank you," she said. "It is so kind of both of you to come and share in our celebration."

"We wouldn't have missed it for the world," said Colon. He turned to Vega. "Martino, could you excuse us for a few minutes? I have some private matters to discuss with Senhora Dominguez."

Vega was momentarily nonplussed by the blunt dismissal, but he recovered quickly. "Why, of course. I see that Rabbi Sasportas has come in. I'll go pay my respects."

"You do that, Martino. I'll find you later. We still have more community business to conclude today."

Vega bowed to Doña Angelica, nodded brusquely to Colon and walked away.

"Senhora, I hope you don't mind that I asked for a little privacy," said Colon. "I am not accustomed to acting as a matchmaker. I know you are busy with the match just concluded, and I must say that they make a beautiful couple. May they provide you with many beautiful grandchildren. But life waits for no one, and there is no time like the present. Someone said that, but I don't recall who it was. No matter. Whoever said it had the right idea. Don't you agree?"

"I do, Senhor Colon, But I have to tell you that —"

"Senhora, let me finish. I know that I sometimes take a little while to get to the point, but I feel that I must say everything that is on my mind in the proper order. I will listen to every word you have to say when I'm finished. Well, where was I? Where was I?"

"You were saying that you were not accustomed to acting as —"

"Ah, yes. Thank you, thank you. Now everything comes back to me. I was saying that your mind is on the match you just concluded — and a very worthy match it is — and that you will not be disposed to listening to suggestions of other matches right here and now, but life waits for no one … and … um … all the rest of that saying. So I want to propose a match to you. Are you willing to listen?"

"You are most kind, Senhor Colon, but I don't think —"

"Senhora Dominguez, the match was not my idea. Rabbi Aboab summoned me and suggested I propose this match to you. Out of respect for the rabbi, I think you should hear me out."

"But Senhor Colon, Sebastian asked me not to listen until — "

"Who said anything about Sebastian, senhora? We are talking about you. Rabbi Aboab asked me to propose this match to you."

"To me!"

"Yes, to you."

Doña Angelica was flustered. "But … I didn't even … I mean … to me!"

"And why not, senhora? You are a gracious lady, still young and full of life. If I didn't know better I would say that you are Felipe's older sister rather than his mother. You've been widowed for over four years. Why should you remain a widow forever? Right now, we're talking about you. Sebastian will find the match he deserves. All in its right time."

"I see," said Doña Angelica. "For me there is no time like the present, but for Sebastian all will take place in its right time."

Colon pulled at his tiny white beard. "Please do not confuse me, senhora. I know that your younger son has become a Talmudic scholar, but must you be one as well? So, what do you say? Will you listen to Rabbi Aboab's suggestion?"

Doña Angelica took a deep breath. She was completely unprepared for something like this, but respect for the rabbi demanded that she at least listen.

"All right," she said. "I'm listening."

Two women came over to wish her congratulations, but Colon dismissed them with a brusque wave of the hand.

"The name the rabbi suggested is Senhor Sergio Setubal," he said. "Do you know of him?"

"I'm afraid not. Does he live here in Amsterdam?"

"Oh, yes. He does. But he is a quiet, unassuming person. He is in his high fifties, tall, fit, very distinguished looking. He is an extremely intelligent man. He attends the rabbi's classes as often as he can, and he donates generously to the community charity funds. And did I mention a very important thing? He is one of the wealthiest Jews in Amsterdam, but hardly anyone would know it. He would never wear the kind of suits I wear — although he would look very good in them, I tell you — and he doesn't ride around in fine carriages, but he is really wealthy, extremely wealthy."

"I gather that he is wealthy."

"You gather correctly, senhora. Pardon me for dwelling so

much on this most minor of his excellent qualities. I know that the Dominguez family is wealthy in its own right. But Senhor Setubal is in a special class of wealth."

"So can you tell me something about his background? Was he …. I mean … what happened to … ?"

"You want to know what happened to his first wife, if there was a first wife. That is, of course, the first question you would be expected to ask. And the answer is, Yes, he had a wife. Senhor Setubal came out of Spain a little over ten years ago. He comes from a prominent Portuguese family in Toledo, mostly Marranos. Senhor Setubal and his wife — I was once told her name but I do not recall it at the moment — lived in Ocaña, a small town between Madrid and Toledo. Actually, the three places would form a triangle, but that's not important right now, is it?"

"No, I don't think it is."

"His wife was taken by the Inquisition, and she died under the torturer's knife. I am told she cried out at the last moment that she was ready to confess if only they would stop the torture. They stopped, but she was too far gone. She died before she could say anything more."

Doña Angelica's eyes misted over with tears, and she bit on her knuckles.

"How tragic," she said.

"Yes, very tragic. But that is the unfortunate experience of our Naçao, our Portuguese Nation. I must apologize for speaking about such a painful subject. I know that it brings bad memories to mind. But I think you had to know the facts. Senhor Setubal managed to escape just a few steps ahead of the Inquisition. He abandoned everything he owned and fled for his life. He hid with relatives in Toledo for a while, and he left the country as soon as he could. He has quite a few relatives here in Amsterdam, too, so he chose to come here."

"Does he have any children?"

"I'm afraid not. His wife was a sickly woman. She never bore him any children."

"And how did he become so wealthy, a recent refugee from Spain?"

"His relatives helped him get set up in business. He is a very astute businessman. I've had dealings with him. I know. Scrupulously honest, truthful and reliable, but clever as a fox. He made his fortune in diamonds."

"So why hasn't he married until now?"

"That is a strange question, senhora, coming from someone who never even considered that I might be proposing a match for her. But I'll answer it anyway. It took him a while to get over the trauma of his terrible experiences in Spain. Then he had to concentrate on establishing himself again financially. A few years ago, he was ready to consider remarriage, but there are not many eligible women of your caliber here, senhora. He entertained a few suggestions, but nothing ever came of it. Rabbi Aboab hopes that this time it will be different."

Doña Angelica dabbed at her brow with a lace handkerchief. "It is getting a little warm in here, I think."

"Yes, it is warm. By the way, Rabbi Aboab made this suggestion primarily out of concern for your welfare. He feels it's time you consider getting married again, and he also feels that Sergio Setubal would be a good choice for you. If it turns out that he is not a perfect match, Rabbi Aboab has other matches in mind. So what do you say? Should I arrange a meeting?"

Doña Angelica nodded somewhat reluctantly, but with a tiny tingle of excitement inside. "Yes, I suppose. This is so unexpected, but in deference to Rabbi Aboab, I should not refuse to see Senhor Setubal."

"Excellent," said Colon. "I will make the arrangements."

He bowed gallantly and went off to mingle some more.

Doña Angelica remained sitting in her place for a few more minutes trying to regain her composure and get control of her jumbled thoughts. A few people came over to congratulate her and chat, but they did not linger when they saw that she appeared distracted. She thought about Don Pedro and the wonderful life they had enjoyed together, but those days were like a distant dream. She reached out in her mind to grab hold of the fading memories.

So much water had passed under the bridge of her life during the previous five years that she felt she was no longer the same person she had been. In Spain, she had been a grand lady who moved easily in the royal palace and the upper echelons of society. She had taken care of her husband and her children, making sure they always had what they needed, and she had run an efficient household with a large household staff. She had entertained often and splendidly, and she had maintained the family's social calendar meticulously.

But she had never worried about the safety of her children. She had never given a thought to money or to the cost of things. She had never kept a budget and scrimped and saved to cover the basic necessities of life. She had never been forced to fight and struggle for the survival of her family. She had never contended with betrayals and false accusations. Life had become very hard for her, but she sensed that she had grown as a person and as a Jewish woman and mother. She now faced the future with new reservoirs of faith, courage, strength and determination. She was confident in her ability to face whatever the future would bring, but she was not sure she could handle a new marriage. Not just yet.

"A guilder for your thoughts, Mother."

Doña Angelica looked up at Sebastian.

"I'm so glad to see you," she said. "You'll never believe what just happened."

The meeting took place three days later at ten o'clock in the evening. As arranged, Eduardo Colon arrived at the Dominguez home together with Sergio Setubal. Felipe was away at the *beis midrash*, but Sebastian remained at home to be with his mother and meet the suitor.

Sergio Setubal was even more impressive than Colon had portrayed him. He was indeed distinguished and well-dressed, but he also had rare elegance and poise. When he came into a room, his presence was immediately felt, even before he did or said anything. His eyes were warm and kind, and they sparkled with quiet intelligence. Sebastian liked him instantly, and he stole a glance at his mother to see how she had reacted. Doña Angelica's face was slightly flushed, but it was not necessarily from excitement; it could have been from nervousness and anxiety. Otherwise, she gave no hint of her feelings.

After pleasantries had been exchanged and the four of them were seated in the parlor, Helga the Norwegian brought in a pot of tea and a bowl of fruit and placed them on a low table.

"Senhor Colon, would you like some tea?" said Doña Angelica, offering to serve the older man first.

"No, thank you, senhora. Perhaps a little later."

"And you, Senhor Setubal?" she said. "Can I offer you a cup of tea?"

"It will be my pleasure, senhora," he said gravely, as if the cup of tea held great significance.

"And how do you like it?" she said. "Would you like some sugar?"

"No, senhora. I like the genuine taste of tea, even if it is a little bitter."

"Funny thing," said Colon. "There was a bit of a frenzy over sugar on the Exchange a little while back. It was all caused by an unfounded rumor about a hurricane in Jamaica.

Senhor Dominguez was there at the time, but I didn't see you there, Senhor Setubal. Did you hear about it?"

Setubal smiled. "Of course. I don't think there is a person in Amsterdam who did not hear about it."

Colon chuckled. "I have no doubt. Anyway, the price collapsed very quickly. But if it had continued to skyrocket I don't know how many households would still be taking sugar with their tea. I think many people would adopt Senhor Setubal's preference for unsweetened tea."

"That might be a good idea anyway," said Doña Angelica. "I have heard that some physicians are not in favor of refined sugar. They say that it makes people fat and that it makes the blood sluggish."

"What do the physicians know?" said Colon. "Today they say this and tomorrow they say something else and the next day something altogether different. I don't think they know what goes on inside the body, because the only time they get a chance to look is when the body is already dead."

"I believe you're being a little harsh on physicians," said Setubal. "No matter how we enjoy deriding them, when we fall ill we run to them for help. Medicine is a science, and it is constantly advancing. And as with all things, when our knowledge broadens, we have to reexamine our old premises. I was not aware of the negative effects of refined sugar, but I shall certainly keep it in mind."

Doña Angelica poured him a cup and placed it in front of him, then she poured for Sebastian and herself. Setubal put his arm over his head to cover it and made a blessing. Then he lifted the cup to his lips, took a small sip and put it back down on the table.

"Delicious," he said. "Perfect flavor. Do you know that in Japan serving tea is an elaborate ritual? Even great samurai warriors consider it an accomplishment to perform a perfect tea ceremony."

"Really?" said Sebastian. "I wonder why."

"I often wondered about that myself, Senhor Dominguez," said Setubal. "It is not so easy to understand the customs of different cultures. I'm sure many people are baffled by a good many of our Jewish customs. But I still would like to attempt an answer to your question. Samurai warriors are men of violence, but they do not consider themselves savage animals. They like to think themselves as highly civilized men of honor and distinction, as men of letters and arts. So they show their talents in the finer points of life by writing poetry and performing delicate tea ceremonies. And then even their performances on the battlefield become forms of their art for them. Does that make any sense?"

Sebastian shrugged. "It does in theory. But as you said, it's hard to relate to that kind of thinking. If I may be so bold, Senhor Setubal, how do you know about tea ceremonies in Japan?"

Setubal gave him a warm smile. "I learn most of what I know from books. I have many of those. Japan is just one of the places I've visited in my reading. You're welcome to stop by anytime you wish and read whatever you like. But I do not lend out my books. Someone once told me not to lend out any books that I intend to keep. Most of them never come back."

"Agreed," said Sebastian. "I will take you up on your offer."

"Please do," said Setubal with full sincerity.

Doña Angelica saw that Colon was starting to fidget. But she was not ready to bring the evening to an end yet.

"Senhor Setubal, do ever feel nostalgia for Spain?" she asked.

A troubled look passed briefly over his face and disappeared. "Well, in Madrid we would be eating dinner about this time," he said, trying to keep his voice light. "That is something I miss. Siestas in the afternoon and dinnertime late at night. But I do not miss the persecution and the fear. No, I do not. But I do feel nostalgia for the home and the life that I had there and lost."

Doña Angelica's hand flew to her mouth. "Oh, I'm so sorry. I didn't mean to open wounds ... oh, I'm sorry ... please forgive me. It was so thoughtless of me."

"There's nothing to forgive, senhora," he said. "We've both suffered tragic losses in that beautiful but terrible country. It may be time to move on."

# THE TOOTHLESS BEGGAR · 8

Zuzarte sat on the stoop of the Dominguez house on the Jodenbreestraat. The sun was still low in the eastern sky, and the heat was bearable. He took a gold watch from his pocket and checked the time. It was still ten minutes to eleven. He considered knocking on the door, but he decided against it. He did not believe in knocking on people's doors before noon at the earliest.

The door finally opened, and Sebastian emerged. Zuzarte stood up and dusted himself off.

"I was getting tired waiting for you, senhor," he said.

"Why didn't you just knock on the door?"

Zuzarte shrugged. "Are you going to the Exchange?"

"I am."

"Do you mind if I walk with you?"

"Not at all. What's on your mind?"

"I would like some of your business," said Zuzarte. "I've been observing your business activities. You have a conservative approach and good judgment, and I think you will be very successful. So I would like to be one of your preferred brokers. I'll bring you deals and give you my opinion, and if you like the deals, you will get the best service from me. And in turn, I will earn a brokerage fee and maybe a little piece of the pie."

"Sounds reasonable. Do you have anything in mind right now?"

They walked past a bakery so crowded that the line formed outside and blocked passage through the street. Sebastian and Zuzarte moved to the left to find a way to get through.

The loud rumble of wagon wheels and the staccato pounding of hooves on the cobblestone streets gave them no more than a second's warning. Zuzarte was quicker than Sebastian to respond. He saw the wagon bearing down on them and instantly flung himself at Sebastian. He pushed him out of the way, and they fell in a heap on the ground. All around them, people scrambled to get out of the way, shouting and screaming as the wagon rolled by and down the street. From his spot on the ground, Sebastian twisted around and tried to catch a glimpse of the wagon driver, but everything was happening too fast. The wagon and its driver disappeared before Sebastian could get a good look at him.

They both stood up and dusted themselves off.

"Are you all right?" said Zuzarte to Sebastian.

"I'm fine. I think I have an injured sleeve, nothing worse. How about you?"

"Nothing. A little scrape on my hand. It's a good thing I heard him at the last second. He would have run both of us down. I mean, we didn't hear him till he was almost on top of us. That means the wagon was going along normally, and then suddenly, it was a mad rush. You know, if it wasn't such a crazy idea, I'd say he was deliberately trying to run us down."

"Why is that such a crazy idea?" said Sebastian.

"Why would someone want to run us down? I don't owe anyone any money right now, and I don't think you do. Why should someone do it?"

"It's not the first time someone has tried to harm me. Or at least that was how it seemed. The other times my assailants wanted something I was carrying, but this time, it seems they wanted to injure or even kill. Believe me, Diego, I don't know who is doing this and what he wants from me."

"Well, I don't know either. So where were we when we were so rudely interrupted? Ah yes, you wanted to know if I have any deals to offer you right now. Actually, I do. There's a nice bit of money to be made in whale oil. The demand is getting stronger. More and more of the common people are using whale oil in their lamps instead of candles to illuminate their homes. There is a shipment coming in soon, and I can get a piece of it. Are you interested?"

"Bring me the numbers, and I'll look at it. Right now, I'm going to make a detour before I go to the Exchange."

Sebastian's detour took him out of the Jewish quarter into a less developed neighborhood called the Plantage, or the Plantation. Little clusters of rough-hewn houses dotted the landscape amidst vegetables gardens and orchards of fruit trees. Here and there, a windmill loomed over its surroundings, its sails turning lazily in the heavy summer air. The streets were thronged with laborers and peddlers. He stopped before a tavern with a sign painted on the front wall that read, "The Toothless Beggar."

There were only a few men inside the tavern, because it was not even noon yet. A lone bartender was drawing a beer for a corpulent man in laborer's overall with black fingernails and a protruding stomach. It was obviously not his first beer of the day, and he tottered on his stool.

The man took one look at Sebastian's feathered hat and sneered.

"Hey, look who's jus' come in," he said to no one in particular, his words slurred and hostile. "A dandy Jew. Have you ever done an honest day's labor in your life, my fine dandy in those fine clothes?"

Sebastian ignored the drunkard and looked around.

"Don't ignore me, Jew," said the drunken laborer. He held up his grime-encrusted hands. "Look at your soft hands, and look at these hands of mine. My hands have worked hard and earned every copper they've received. Those black stains will never come off, but these hands — my hands! — are clean. Really clean. Can you say the same for yours?"

"Be quiet, Henryk," said a voice from a table in a dark corner of the room. "This man is my friend. If you pester him, you will not be welcome to come back here any more."

The man muttered something under his breath and turned his attention back to his beer.

"Come, sit here with me, Don Sebastian," said Gonzalo. He was lounging in a captain's chair with a glass of wine in one hand and a smoking pipe in the other. "Don't mind Henryk Stuyvesant. He's a cousin to Peter Stuyvesant, who used to be governor of New Amsterdam, before it became New York. Peter Stuyvesant was a real hater of Jews, so Henryk here thinks it's his obligation to follow in the family tradition. But he's really harmless. Anyway, what brings you here in the middle of the day? How come you're not at the Exchange?"

"A wagon just tried to run me down while I was walking in the street."

Gonzalo sat up straight. "Tell me about it."

"That's all there is to tell. I was walking down the street with a friend, when suddenly a wagon came bearing down on us at full speed. If my friend hadn't knocked me out of the way, the wagon probably would have hit both of us."

"Did you get a description of the driver?"

"No. It happened too fast."

"This is serious. Whoever is behind this has decided to do you harm and not just steal your papers. What happened to change his mind, whoever he is?"

"I don't know, Gonzalo. I'm completely in the dark. It's as if I'm fighting a phantom. Or at least, I would like to fight the phantom if he would show himself. But even though I can't see him, I can actually feel the hatred coming at me."

"So what's on your mind?" said Gonzalo. "You've come

here with a plan, and I'm at your service. Would you like something to drink?"

"A glass of water would be fine."

He snapped his fingers at the bartender. "Roelof, a glass of water for my guest." Gonzalo turned back to Sebastian. "That's Roelof Groesbeck. I think I once mentioned him to you. He and his wife Trijntje take care of this house, the tavern, my apartment upstairs and the rooms I rent out in the back. During the day, he fills in as my bartender. He's a lucky find for me. He just walked in one day like a messenger from Heaven and asked if I needed someone to manage the tavern and the property. I'm fortunate to have him."

The bartender brought Sebastian a large glass of water. He nodded curtly and walked away.

"All right, we can talk."

"I have to find this phantom, Gonzalo. But I don't even know where to begin to look. In the meantime, I'm in danger, and my family's in danger. More so after today than before. An attack might come at any time and from any direction. We need protection. I want you to hire bodyguards for the three of us — my mother, my brother and me — but I want them to stay out of sight. I'll pay what it costs, but I need good surveillance for the foreseeable future."

Gonzalo scratched his head. "Let me think a minute. Let's see ... All right, I can use Piet Vanderweghe, he's a tough fellow. And Roelof Groesbeck could help out when an extra pair of hands is needed. And ... yes, we'll have the bodyguards in place by this evening and some people to watch the house during the night. It won't cost you too much. These men owe me some favors. I'll get them to charge you a fair price."

"Then that's settled," said Sebastian. "I can breathe a little more easily now."

He took a sip of water and wiped his lips. Out of the corner of his eye, he saw a figure dressed in black watching him through a window. He turned to face the window, but the figure was gone. He could not be sure if it had been a man or a woman, but he was certain someone had been watching him drink his water.

"I think I was followed here, Gonzalo," he said.

"It's possible. Are you going to the Exchange from here?"

"Yes. That's what I was planning to do."

"Give me two minutes," said Gonzalo, "and I'll have one of my men trail behind you. If you're being followed, he'll catch the follower and bring him here. Maybe we'll get some information out of him."

Gonzalo got up and left the room through a small door in the back. He returned in two minutes, as he had promised.

"It's all arranged," he said.

"Excellent. Well, I'm off. By the way, how's your Dutch doing, Gonzalo?"

"Not bad. I know about thirty words. Covers everything I need most of the time. When things get hot and I have to say something more … elaborate, I say it in Spanish. Strange, but everyone seems to understand."

"One more thing before I go," said Sebastian. "Why's your tavern called The Toothless Beggar?"

"That'll have to remain my secret for a while."

Sebastian stood up. He shook hands with Gonzalo. The two men nodded at each other. There was no need for additional words.

Walking back through the Plantage, Sebastian kept looking over his shoulder to see if he was being followed. Once, he thought he saw someone duck into an alleyway, but he couldn't know if it was Gonzalo's man or a stalker.

The trading hours were almost over when he reached the Exchange. Zuzarte was deep in conversation with a Tudesco trader; when he saw Sebastian he waved and signaled with one finger that he would be right over. Sebastian was not in the mood of trading, especially with the Exchange about to close for the day. He would have wanted to go home, but he waited for Zuzarte.

"You look a little pale," said Zuzarte when he finally extricated himself from the other trader. "That fellow I was talking to when you came in? He's trying to get me interested in dried bananas from Brazil. He insists that dried bananas will be all the rage in Amsterdam and the rest of Europe within months."

"And what do you think?"

"Dried bananas? I don't think so. I'm always looking for some really hot commodity that has not yet become popular. If we could invest in something surefire we would really do well. I mean, very, very well."

Sebastian nodded. "But it's not dried bananas."

"No. When it comes, I will recognize it. In the meantime, I recommend a moderate investment in whale oil."

"As I said —"

"Yes, I didn't forget. You wanted the numbers. I have them here for you."

Sebastian considered the offer and decided to accept it. It was a moderately conservative investment, and he would be out of it in fewer than three weeks.

The closing bell sounded, and Sebastian took his leave from Zuzarte and went home by way of Amos Strasbourg's office. They discussed the situation for over an hour, but they could not come up with anything of value. The only positive development was that Netzach Tomashov had made some headway in finding Karl and Steen. Some dockhands in Rotterdam recalled a pair of mercenaries who went by those names arriving on a ship from Brazil over a year earlier. It was not much, but it was a start.

Amos accompanied Sebastian part of the way home, and they chatted amiably as they walked. Then Amos returned to his office and Sebastian walked alone the rest of the way to the Jodenbreestraat.

A man in a dark suit was waiting for him on the stoop of the house.

"Are you Senhor Dominguez?" he asked.

"I am."

"You are summoned to the Maamad."

"For what?"

"I couldn't say, senhor. I'm just a messenger."

"Very well. When do they want me to come?"

"Right now, senhor."

"You mean today?" asked Sebastian.

"I mean right now. You are to come with me."

"May I go inside and have a drink of water?"

"Of course, senhor. I will wait right here."

"Never mind," said Sebastian. "Let's go."

Five *parnassim* of the Maamad were waiting for him in the spacious room the Maamad used for its meetings and hearings. He was already acquainted with three of them.

Before the hearing got under way, Eduardo Colon called Sebastian aside and said to him in a low voice. "Senhor Dominguez, Senhor Setubal was pleased with the meeting with your mother and would like to meet again, at your mother's convenience, of course. But I have not yet heard a response from your mother. Could you please encourage her to respond soon, and favorably?"

"I will speak to her. In the meantime, could you tell me why I was called down here?"

"I cannot tell you, but you will find out momentarily."

The session began with some formal preliminaries. The *parnassim* sat at a long table in front of the room, and Sebastian was asked to stand in front of them. Colon addressed the issue.

"Senhor Dominguez," he said, "we have had a disturbing

report earlier today, and we have called you here to confirm or deny the accusations."

"Accusations?" echoed Sebastian. "What accusations?"

"If you recall," said Colon, "we did tell you that, according to the rules of the Naçao, the members of the Portuguese community may not fraternize with gentiles, except for employees and business associates."

"I recall."

"Well, you were seen today in a tavern in the Plantage called …" Colon paused to consult a paper. "Yes, it is called The Toothless Beggar. The names people choose for taverns are beyond me. I don't know why they can't call them something normal. But I suppose people who want to go and get drunk are intrigued by ridiculous names of that sort. In any case, you were seen in that tavern, sitting at a table with a large gentile man and drinking together. The gentile was drinking red wine, according to our report, and you were drinking some clear liquor. Arak perhaps."

"Do you deny these charges?" asked Martino Vega.

"Honored gentlemen," said Sebastian, "I do not deny that I was in that tavern today, but it is not as you think. I was not drinking arak. It was plain water. The man at the table with me was Gonzalo Sanchez, one of my father's trusted retainers. Gonzalo has been with me all my life. He helped me escape from prison in Spain. He almost helped me escape from prison in Vienna, if a cannonball hadn't collapsed the wall. He also saved my life in the Black Forest on the way back from Vienna to Metz."

Colon cleared his throat. "I understand your longstanding relationship with this man, but we still disapprove of a member of our community drinking with gentiles in a tavern in the Plantage. Even if you were drinking water. I do not know what business you have with him now, but why do you have to meet with him in a tavern of all places?"

"The tavern belongs to Gonzalo," said Sebastian. "He lives upstairs. This morning, I was almost run down deliberately by a wagon on the Jodenbreestraat. Someone is out to do me harm. I went to ask Gonzalo to arrange protection for my mother, my brother and myself."

"That is a shocking story," said Colon. He looked to his colleagues, and they nodded. "We are all agreed that the charges should be dropped. You did exactly as you should have done. But in the future, please avoid that tavern as much as possible. If someone should see you going in there, they could get the wrong idea. So meet with your man in other places, if there is time to arrange it."

"I will keep that in mind. And can I ask a question of you?"

"Certainly. I don't promise to answer, but you can ask."

"Who told you about my visit to The Toothless Beggar?"

"The report came in a letter delivered by a messenger."

"Was there a signature?"

"No. The letter was anonymous."

# BITTER MUD · 9

ZUZARTE WAS TALKING ANIMATEDLY with a Turkish trader in a long white robe and a brown turban. Out of the corner of his eye, he caught sight of Sebastian entering the trading floor of the Exchange, and he greeted him with a wave and a big smile without interrupting his conversation with the Turk. Sebastian returned the greeting and went to his accustomed place of business under the portico.

Over the next half hour, brokers offered Sebastian shares in a shipload of dried figs from Morocco, a packet of pearls from Margarita Island off the coast of Venezuela and a rooming house in the Dutch city of Utrecht. He listened politely and promised to get back to them if he should have any interest in these investments. He also took note of the activity in sugar. Prices were rising, but he was not prepared to invest any money in it.

Presently, Zuzarte concluded his business with the Turk and came over to Sebastian. "You're looking well," he said. "Looking at you, no one would know that just yesterday you'd almost been killed or badly injured."

"You mean, of course," said Sebastian, "because my clothes are clean."

"You can make light of it, but I think it's a serious thing. A very serious thing. Did you find out anything about who was behind this?"

"No. But I'm working on it."

"Well, the quicker you find out the better."

"I can't argue with that," said Sebastian. "So, I saw you talking to that Turkish fellow for a long time. Anything interesting?"

"You mean as far as business opportunities?"

"Yes."

"There may be," said Zuzarte, "but before I bring you a deal, I'm going to check it out thoroughly myself. In the meantime, I do have some small deals to offer you. Better ones than dried bananas from Brazil."

Zuzarte proceeded to offer Sebastian a variety of deals, most of which promised moderate profits with low risk. The most exciting of the deals, however, involved shares in a new diamond mine in Africa. There was an opportunity here for quite substantial profits should the mine live up to expectation, but the risk factor was also higher.

"It's a really sweet deal," said Zuzarte. "The company needs money to develop the mine, and they're selling the shares for a very good price. I know this is a little too risky for your tastes, Senhor Dominguez, but I don't really think this is like gambling. It's a new diamond mine. The experts say it's going to be a good one, and we have a chance to get in on the ground floor. I'm not telling you to say yes right away. Just think about it, and check it out a little on your own."

"I'll do that."

"Good. In the meantime, I'll keep my eyes and ears open. As I always do."

*The obvious person to ask about the diamond mine*, thought Sebastian as soon as Zuzarte had gone off to search for new opportunities and new clients, *was Sergio Setubal*. Sebastian was sure he would get good information and advice from the older man, but he felt uncomfortable approaching him before his mother decided whether or not to see him again. Sebastian had tried to bring up the subject the night before, as Eduardo

Colon had asked him to do, but it had not been possible. Doña Angelica had hosted a charitable function in the house, and some of the ladies had lingered late into the night, long after Sebastian had retired for the night. And today when he came back for breakfast after Shacharis, she was already off on a round of errands. Helga the Norwegian could not say where she had gone and when she would return.

The closing bell rang, and Sebastian headed back home. Once again, he kept looking over his shoulder to see if anyone was stalking him and if he could pick out his bodyguards from the crowd. He was unsuccessful on both counts.

Doña Angelica was having tea in the parlor with an old lady when Sebastian came home. Fifteen minutes later, the visitor was gone.

"So how was your day?" Doña Angelica said brightly.

Sebastian could see that his mother's good cheer was a little forced, as if she had something on her mind. He decided to let her tell it to him in her own good time.

"My day was fine," he said. "How was yours?"

"Just wonderful. I don't think I've ever been so busy in my life. So many committee meetings. So many projects. And the preparations for Felipe's wedding! Why, he's going to get married before Chanukah, and I've hardly done anything yet." She paused. "And I have some good news, Sebastian."

"Really? What is it?"

"I received a letter this morning."

"Please don't keep me in suspense, Mother."

"The letter was from Hamburg."

"From Carolina?" said Sebastian. "She's coming to Felipe's wedding. That is really good news. I haven't seen my little sister in a year."

"No, I'm afraid she's not coming, but it's for a good reason. She had a baby."

"A baby! Carolina's a mother?"

"Yes!" said Doña Angelica, and she clapped her hands with delight. "Thank the Almighty, Carolina has a healthy baby. She's a mother. You're an uncle. And me, I'm a grandmother! I can't believe it. And I didn't even know she was expecting! I suppose she didn't want me to worry."

"Or else she thought you'd be on the next boat to Hamburg. Not that she wouldn't have wanted to see you. But knowing Carolina, she didn't want to put you through all the effort of an arduous journey. I'm sure she could have used your help, but she was more concerned about you than about herself."

"Yes, I suppose you're right. Carolina was always a good child."

"So don't keep me in suspense, Mother. Tell me something. Was it a boy or a girl? Does the baby have a name? What does the baby look like? Details. Give me details."

"It's a boy, Sebastian! A boy! And his name is Akiva, named after your father, may he rest in peace in Gan Eden. It's the name they gave him posthumously in Metz because he died to sanctify the Name. Carolina and Uriel have decided not to give him a Spanish or Portuguese name. So it's just Akiva, the Hebrew name. Like his father Uriel and his grandfather Boaz. Akiva Pereira! I just love the name. It has such a nice ring to it. Carolina writes that he's a big, strong boy with a full head of black hair and the biggest blue eyes you've ever seen. She says he likes to cry a lot, but he calms down when she sings to him. She wrote me such a beautiful letter. Read it. It's on the dining room table."

"I will, Mother. There's something else I wanted to discuss with you. I wanted to talk about it last night, but you had company."

"I know what you want, Sebastian. You want to know what I intend to do about Senhor Setubal. He wants us to meet again. Did you know that?"

"Yes, Mother. Senhor Colon told me. He hasn't heard from you."

"So what do you think?"

"How can I tell you what to do, Mother?"

""I'm just a little confused right now, Sebastian. I would like to hear your thoughts on the matter."

"Mother, I want you to be happy. You're so young and full of life. You have to think of the future. Felipe is going to get married soon, and one of these days I will think of getting married myself. And then you'll be living all by yourself. Just you and Helga the Norwegian."

"So you think I should get married?"

"Yes, I do. I think that Father would want you to get married. How long can you be in mourning? We're settled here in Amsterdam and quite well established. It's time to put the past behind us and move on. And I think Senhor Setubal is a good choice."

"You like him, don't you?'

"Yes, I like him. He is a very fine person. And he is warm and caring. What more can you want?"

"You didn't mention his fabulous wealth."

"Mother, I would favor the match even if Senhor Setubal was penniless."

"No, I think it's good that he is independent," said Doña Angelica. "I wouldn't want him to rely on my money to get us by."

"So are you saying that you want to see him again?"

"I ... I'm just not sure what I want."

"What are your reservations, Mother?"

Doña Angelica bit her lower lip. "I'm just not sure if I'm ready to get married just yet. You say that everything is settled and that we should look toward the future. But I don't feel so settled. How can I forget about the past when we're being stalked and persecuted? Someone is out to do us harm, you in particular. Who betrayed you in Vienna and tried to get you sent back to Spain? Who attempted to have me tried for witchcraft? Who attacked you in the Black Forest and again here in Amsterdam? I agree with you, Sebastian, that Senhor Setubal would be a fine choice for a husband, and he would be a kind and considerate stepfather for my children. But how can I think of marriage before we resolve these questions that hang over us like a dark cloud?"

"I understand, Mother. But look at the other side. If you say no to Senhor Setubal, he will move on, and that will be the end of it. And if we resolve the questions within a few weeks — which I hope and pray will happen — it will be too late to change your mind. So I would suggest you agree to see him again, and when you meet, be honest with him. Tell him what your concerns are and explain to him that you need a little time. Ask him to be patient with you. He seems to be a patient man. He will understand."

Doña Angelica nodded. "Makes a lot of sense, Sebastian. I won't answer at the moment, but I will think about it seriously and answer very soon."

"Is part of your reluctance that you are nervous about starting a new life?"

"Yes, it is. It is not easy to close the book on the past."

"I understand, Mother."

"Do you really? You will never have to close the book on your father the way I will have to close the book on him when I remarry."

"I know, Mother. But still. Life must go on."

"Yes, it must. So let's talk about your life now."

"Mine?" said Sebastian.

"Yes, yours. You are thirty-one years old. It's time you got married."

"I agree, Mother. I'll be ready as soon as I get my life completely in order."

Doña Angelica laughed. "So it's all right for you to say that, but not for me?"

"It's not the same, Mother. You have to decide about Senhor Setubal."

"And you have to make a decision about Dulce Castillo."

"Dulce Castillo? Who is Dulce Castillo?"

"That sweet old lady who was here when you came in? That was Senhora Belinfante. She was here two days ago and suggested a match for you. I didn't tell you about it until I looked into it carefully. What was the point of telling you? But I did look into it. Quite a bit, actually. Do you want to listen?"

"Out of respect for you, Mother, I will listen."

"It is not such bitter medicine, Sebastian. Dulce Castillo is a marvelous young woman in every way. She is eighteen years old, mature for her age, charming, personable and very intelligent. I've met her, and I have no doubt that you will enjoy her company. She is a sophisticated young woman, and she will be an interesting companion to you for your whole life. And she comes from a fine family. Her father, Senhor Miguel Castillo, is involved in community affairs. He is being considered for one of the *parnas* positions on the Maamad, a much respected man. Her mother, Senhora Maite Castillo, is active in most of the important charities. The Castillo family is not fabulously wealthy, but they are among the wealthier members of the Nação. Senhor Castillo has many investments, and they say that he is quite a Torah scholar, almost a rabbi. Dulce has two older brothers, both of whom are married and have young children. She is the youngest child, pampered but not spoiled."

"So what do you want me to say, Mother?"

"I want you to agree to a meeting."

Sebastian closed his eyes and leaned his forehead on his right hand. In all fairness, his mother was right. He was urging her to look toward the future even though the past was not yet completely resolved, and she had every right to expect the same from him. And at thirty-one years old, it really was about time that he considered getting married. He took a deep breath and looked up.

"Has she agreed to see me?"

"Not officially, because you must give the first response. But Senhora Belinfante assures me — unofficially, of course — that the Castillo family would be favorably disposed to you if they were officially approached."

"All right, Mother. I agree to a meeting."

A radiant smile spread across Doña Angelica's face. "You've made me so happy, Sebastian. I am so excited! Imagine how wonderful it would be if you, Felipe and I were all married before the winter is over."

Sebastian smiled uneasily. "Yes, that would really be something."

"And Carolina has a little boy. You know, we've been through so much in the last few years, but perhaps our fortunes are finally turning around. Perhaps the Almighty has finally decided that we've suffered enough."

"I certainly hope so, Mother."

"Oh, if only we could find out —"

She was interrupted by a tentative knock on the door. Helga the Norwegian stuck her head into the room. "I am sorry to disturb you, madame. There is a man at the door."

"Did he tell you his name?" said Doña Angelica.

"Yes. He said it was Diego Zuzarte."

"Show him in, Helga."

Helga's head disappeared and the door closed.

"Who is this man?" said Doña Angelica.

"It's a friend of mine, Mother. From the Exchange."

There was slight tap on the door, and Zuzarte came into the room. He was carrying a little burlap sack.

"Senhora Dominguez, it is a great honor," he said with a chivalrous bow.

"Senhor Zuzarte." She rose. "I will leave you men to talk business."

"No, please don't go," said Zuzarte. "I have brought something to show Sebastian, and it would really be helpful if you saw it too."

Doña Angelica sat back down, intrigued. "What do you want to show us?"

"I will show it to you in a few minutes," said Zuzarte. "I asked your housekeeper to put up a pot of water, and as soon as it is ready I will make the demonstration."

"What are you talking about, Diego?" said Sebastian.

"I'm talking about coffee," said Zuzarte. "Are you familiar with coffee?"

"It is a medicine, isn't it? They sell in the apothecary shop. I think it's supposed to be good for irregularity and other problems of the digestion."

Zuzarte shook his head. "That all may be true. But more than anything else, coffee is a drink. It is very popular in Turkey and the Arab countries. And it looks as if it's going to be coming to Europe soon in a very big way. It is starting to catch on all over the continent. Here, let me show you." He pulled a handful of beans from the burlap sack he had brought with him. "These are coffee beans. If you grind them and cook them, they make a potent drink."

"Do you mean like wine or liquor?" said Sebastian.

"Not at all. I will give you a taste in a few minutes, and you'll tell me what you think." He reached into the sack again and pulled out a folded cloth. He opened the cloth to reveal a thick brown powder. "This is coffee ground into a powder. You cook this powder and drink the broth."

Helga appeared at the door. "The water is boiling," she announced to no one in particular. "I will be upstairs."

Zuzarte looked at Doña Angelica. "Do you mind if go into the kitchen?"

"Not at all," she replied. "In fact, we'll all go into the kitchen and continue this experiment there. Helga is straightening the upstairs bedrooms. We will have privacy."

"I hope Helga doesn't come down," said Sebastian, "and imagine that we are brewing up some magic potions."

Doña Angelica gave him a stern look. "That is not amusing, Sebastian."

Twenty minutes later, Zuzarte poured a deep brown viscous liquid into three earthenware bowls. He gave one each to Doña Angelica and Sebastian and took the third for himself. He closed his eyes and made the blessing, then he lifted the bowl to his lips and took a few sips.

"Ah," he sighed with pleasure.

Doña Angelica was the next to take a sip. Her face immediately became contorted into a grimace, but she was too ladylike to spit it out. She swallowed whatever was in her mouth and shuddered.

"Horrible," she gasped. "It's like drinking bitter mud."

"Indeed, it is," said Zuzarte. "But in a few minutes you will feel something extraordinary. How about you, Sebastian? Are you brave enough to try it?"

Sebastian picked up his bowl and took a few sips. The coffee had cooled somewhat by then, so he continued to drink until he had emptied the bowl.

"I'm proud of you," said Zuzarte. "You took it like a man. Swallowed the whole thing without any complaints. So how was it?"

"Vile stuff," said Sebastian. "It is bitter mud, as my mother described it."

"Some people sweeten it," said Zuzarte, "to take the edge off the bitterness, but I like it exactly as it is. My Turkish friend — the one to whom I was speaking at the Exchange —

he suggested that I try it. So I did. I've been experimenting with coffee for several weeks now, and I love it."

"But the taste, senhor!" said Doña Angelica. "How can you bring yourself to drink bitter mud?"

"When the rewards are high enough," said Zuzarte, "the taste is unimportant. Could I trouble you to take a little more, senhora? The coffee has cooled."

Doña Angelica grimaced and held her nose, but she gamely picked up the bowl and took a long drink. She shuddered again and said, "Would you say that I took it like a man?"

"Like a gallant lady, senhora," said Zuzarte. "Now let us just sit here for a few minutes and chat while the coffee takes effect."

The conversation started languidly as they discussed politics and other trivial matters. But within minutes, the conversation grew animated and even heated.

"What is going on?" said Doña Angelica, suddenly aware of the change in the tenor of the conversation. "I feel as if the blood is racing through my veins faster than ever before. Everything around me seems sharper and brighter. Do you feel the same things, Sebastian?"

"Oh, yes," he said. "And more. I feel that my head is clearer than I ever remember. My thoughts are like flying daggers, sharp and whistling through the air to find their targets unerringly. What kind of a drink is this?"

"It is coffee, my friend," said Zuzarte. "The secret was hidden for a long time in the casbahs and souks of the Muslim world, but now it is coming out. It is the elixir of kings and princes. But soon it will be in the mouths of all people. And those that have the vision and foresight will make their fortunes in this wonderful, golden, bitter mud."

Doña Angelica lifted her bowl and drained it to the last drop. She shuddered again. "Brrh, bitter! But I want some more. Is there anything left in the pot?"

"I can cook up some more," said Zuzarte.

"Please do," said Doña Angelica.

Zuzarte poured some more of the thick powder into the pot. When the brew was ready, he refilled the three bowls.

Doña Angelica held the bowl under her nose and sniffed at the steam rising from the liquid. "Ah," she breathed. "This is a wonderful aroma, but I wish the taste wasn't so bitter."

"You can do something to take the edge off the bitterness," said Zuzarte. "I've heard that in Morocco and other places they put in a lot of sugar. And I also heard that some people put in milk. If you want, you can try either of those methods. Or even both together. But I don't want any of those things. I want to make sure that the power of the drink is not diluted."

The three of them drank their coffee without adding anything to mitigate the bitterness. Then they sat back to savor the contentment.

Zuzarte refolded the cloth in which the ground coffee was wrapped and slipped it into the burlap sack.

"So have you changed your minds about coffee?" he said.

"I've made a complete turnaround," said Sebastian.

"So have I," said Doña Angelica. "Er … Senhor Zuzarte … could you leave some of that powder with us? I would like to experiment with it some more."

Zuzarte laughed. He pulled the folded cloth from the sack and placed it on the table. "You can have all of it, senhora. Experiment to your heart's content."

"You are most kind, senhor. I believe you and Sebastian want to talk a little business. You can speak in the parlor. I must stay here and supervise the preparations for dinner, so I will not disturb you. Would you like to stay for dinner, Senhor Zuzarte?"

"I would love to stay," he said. "But my wife is expecting me."

"Another time, then," she said.

She went off to find Helga, and the two men returned to the parlor.

"What did you think?" said Zuzarte. "Have we got a tiger by the tail here?"

"It would seem so. I agree that coffee will become the most popular drink in Amsterdam, perhaps in all of Europe. But how do you suggest we profit from it?"

"I'll tell you what I've worked out," said Zuzarte, "but I want your assurance that you'll help me profit from this venture as well. I am not a rich man. I make a living, yes, and not a bad one. But in no way could you consider me rich. I'd like to be rich, so if I help you become richer I want you to help me become rich."

"What do you mean exactly?"

"When you get into the coffee trade, I want to be your exclusive broker, and I want you to give me an additional percentage point for my commission. I think that is fair."

Sebastian nodded. "So do I. But why are you coming to me? Why don't you bring this deal that you are putting together to someone much richer than I am?"

"Because I don't trust them," said Zuzarte. "They will cast me aside as soon as the market heats up. I cannot expect loyalty from the big traders. But I trust you, Senhor Dominguez. You strike me as an honorable man, and I am willing to stake my fortune — my future fortune — on it."

"Fair enough," said Sebastian. "I'm flattered that you consider me trustworthy and honorable. I try to be both of those things. So what's the deal?"

"The deal," said Zuzarte, "is this. There is some light trading in coffee, but for the most part, there is not much activity. Right now the price of coffee is at sixty-four, which is moderate but not too expensive. According to my information, it will soon go up sharply."

"And your information is …?"

"The Turk is bringing a ship called *Java Moon* to Amsterdam from Djakarta on the island of Java in the Dutch East Indies. The ship is loaded with high-quality coffee, the bitterest mud you'll ever taste. It will be arriving in two months or thereabouts. This information is not known to the market. The Turk has arranged that prominent people will be introduced to the bitter mud in the next few weeks, as your mother was, so demand will be very strong. It seems to me that your mother will be one of the first on line to stock up on the beans."

Sebastian chuckled. "I think you may be right."

"I'm sure of it, but she'll have plenty of people pushing to get ahead of her. Anyway, when the coffee arrives, there will be a frenzy of buying, and the price will skyrocket. It could easily go above two hundred or even higher."

"Go on."

"The Turk needs money now. So he is keeping a large percentage of the shipment for himself and he is selling shares in the rest of it. The cost of the shares is based on the going price of coffee today. So we can buy into this ship and when the price goes up we will make a fortune. I am putting a thousand guilders of my own money into the deal, and I would like you to put in at least thirty thousand guilders, part of which will go toward my commission."

"Thirty thousand guilders! That is a lot of money."

"Yes, it is."

"Let me think about it overnight," said Sebastian. "I will give you my answer in the morning."

# THE MYSTERIOUS CLIENT · 10

COFFEE OCCUPIED MOST OF SEBASTIAN'S THOUGHTS for the next week, although a great many important things were going on in his life. Doña Angelica met again with Sergio Setubal. Eduardo Colon and Sebastian were present at the meeting, as before, but they participated in the conversation as little and as politely possible. The conversation progressed beyond pleasantries and trivialities, turning to more serious matters of a spiritual and financial nature.

The prospects for the match brightened, but still, there was no commitment on either side. Setubal readily agreed to a third meeting, and Doña Angelica consented after taking two days to think about it.

Meanwhile, the Castillo family agreed to consider Sebastian as a match for their daughter Dulce, and a tentative meeting was arranged. Sebastian gave some thought to the possible topics of conversation he would raise with her, but time and again, he found his mind drifting back to his bold adventure in coffee.

During the days after his purchase of coffee shares, he and Zuzarte monitored the prices very closely. There was some slight fluctuation up and down, but nothing to cause any alarm. On one occasion when the price dipped for a few hours, Sebastian bought some more shares on the open market.

On the day of the appointed meeting with Dulce Castillo, Zuzarte sought him out at the Exchange. The broker was uncharacteristically worried.

"We have trouble, senhor," he said. "A broker named Coronal is dumping a large block of coffee shares on the market. He's asking fifty-two so that he can sell the shares quickly. If he does that, he could drive down the price of coffee."

"But won't it go up when *Java Moon* comes in from the East Indies?"

"Not necessarily. If the bottom drops out of the market now and there's panic selling, no one will be interested in the coffee when it comes into port. We have to stop him from dumping the coffee."

"This Coronal is a broker. Whom does he represent? Who's the real seller?"

"I don't know. He won't say."

"Do you have any idea?"

"I suspect it may be Johannes Hoogaboom, the director of the Bank of Amsterdam, but I can't be sure."

"What's your basis for your suspicion?"

"I saw them talking together yesterday."

"That's all?" said Sebastian.

"It was enough for me. Coronal is bit of an unsavory character. He doesn't usually talk to directors of banks."

"Well, I can't very well approach Hoogaboom based on that alone. Can you ask Coronal to get his client to hold off? Explain to him that he stands to gain much profit if he's patient for a little while longer."

"You think I didn't try that? It's no use. His client wants the money right now. He's not interested in waiting. The only thing we can do is buy it ourselves. Fifty-two is a very good price."

"I don't want to buy any more coffee shares, Diego. I have more than enough right now."

"Absolutely. I agree with you, but what are we supposed to do? If he dumps his coffee shares, the price will drop, and we'll take a big loss. You'll take a bigger loss than I will, but my thousand guilders mean as much to me as your thirty thousand guilders mean to you. I can't really afford to lose my money. I have a family to support."

Sebastian brooded for a while, his eyebrows knitted together in concentration. "I feel trapped," he said at last. "But I suppose there's nothing else I can do. I'll go to the bank to get the money. In the meantime, make the arrangements with Coronal. Who knows? This may turn out to be a blessing in disguise."

A clamp of anxiety gripped Sebastian's heart as he walked to the Bank of Amsterdam. Unaccustomed to the perils of speculation, he did not know how to navigate these uncharted waters. Had he made a serious mistake in speculating in coffee? Had his infatuation with the exotic bean clouded his better judgment? Lost in his thoughts, he did not see the nondescript man emerge from the bank.

"Good day, Senhor Dominguez," said Yakob Santos. "I hope you're well."

"Good day to you, Senhor Santos," he replied mechanically. "Do you come here often?"

"No," said Santos. He gave him an odd look, tipped his hat and walked away.

Johannes Hoogaboom, the director, greeted Sebastian cordially. His wife Wilhelmina sat in her accustomed place, her nose buried in piles of documents.

"So how is it going, Senhor Dominguez?" said Hoogaboom.

"Quite well," said Sebastian. "I've come to make a withdrawal." He named the figure.

"We're never happy with substantial withdrawals," said Hoogaboom, "but in this case, I am more than a little concerned. I've heard you've been speculating. I didn't think that was your method."

"It was not really speculation," said Sebastian. "Just a

little higher risk than usual. I have every confidence in my investment."

"Well, it's your money, Senhor Dominguez. But be extra careful."

Sebastian returned to the Exchange with the money. He expected Zuzarte to be happy to see him, but the broker seemed crestfallen.

"What's the matter, Diego?" he said.

"Trouble with Coronal. I told him I would buy his shares. So he told me the price had gone up to fifty-seven."

"But he offered at fifty-two," protested Sebastian. He was angry. "He can't change his mind."

"I'm afraid he can. If we'd accepted his offer right away, he'd be committed. But we didn't, so he has the right to withdraw the offer or change the price."

"So what are our choices? Can we just withdraw our own offer and forget about it? He's selling for a higher price. The market won't collapse."

"That's what's so diabolical about what this Coronal is doing. His price is low enough to collapse the market, but high enough to strain our resources."

"So we have to pay his price."

"Believe me, I don't want to do it. But what choice do we have? If we don't, we may take a big loss."

"All right," said Sebastian. "Buy it, but I must find out who is behind this."

"I agree. This person may continue doing this again and again until he bleeds us dry."

Sebastian walked home from the Exchange in a red haze. His feelings swung like a pendulum from fear of failure and disgrace to anger and frustration with himself and the situation in general. He hardly gave a thought to the meeting that would take place in the Castillo home in a few hours or to the young woman who might one day become his wife.

When he came home, however, Doña Angelica's excitement at the forthcoming meeting lifted his spirits. He had two bowls of coffee and some cheese, and he relaxed. Two hours later, his nerves had calmed somewhat, and he was able to put business matters aside and focus on the meeting.

Dulce Castillo turned out to be everything she was said to be and more. At the meeting, Sebastian and Doña Angelica sat on one side of the dining room table and Dulce sat with her parents on the other side. A bowl of fruit stood in the middle of the table, but no one touched any of it. The conversation flowed easily, and the atmosphere was convivial.

After about an hour, the Castillos offered to show Doña Angelica their art collection, especially their prized Rembrandts and Vermeers hanging in the salon. Sebastian and Dulce were left alone for a brief time.

"Aren't you curious to see the Rembrandts and Vermeers?" she asked with a mischievous twinkle in her eyes.

"Perhaps another time," said Sebastian.

"That would be nice. So I hear that you are a trader."

"I don't think of myself as a trader. It's just something I do for a few hours a day. It's not what I am."

"So what are you then?"

Sebastian felt a knot in his throat. In one brief sentence, this charming young woman had penetrated the confusion and insecurity that lay at the bottom of his heart. Who was he? In Spain, he had been a prince and a secret Jew, two identities that he had embraced simultaneously, two identities that had given him satisfaction and fulfillment. But what was his identity now? Felipe had found his perfect identity. He knew what he was, who he was and where he intended to go. But he himself was floundering, groping, inwardly lost.

"Your question, senhorita," he said, "is like an arrow that flies through the air and finds its mark perfectly. And the answer I am about to give you is sincere and true, not just something to say. You want to know what I am. I am a lost Jew seeking to find his way back to the Almighty, but I don't know how."

Dulce smiled at him. "I love your answer. It is the purest of the pure. I am so sorry that you are suffering, but I'm sure that one day you'll find what you seek."

Sebastian felt as if a stone had been lifted from his heart.

During the week after the meeting in the Castillo home, Sebastian looked back at that fateful day with amazement at how darkness could turn to light so quickly. The day had started off with the crisis of Coronal's coffee shares, and it had ended with the real possibility that he had found the wife who was destined for him from the moment she was born.

After that evening, fortune smiled on the Dominguez family. The Castillos agreed to a second meeting. Doña Angelica consented to see Sergio Setubal for a third time. Preparations for Felipe's wedding were progressing smoothly. And the coffee market stabilized.

Slowly and almost imperceptibly, the price of coffee began to rise. Sebastian was very heavily invested in coffee, but his shares were now worth more than he had paid for them. He would have loved nothing more than to sell off his shares, take a modest profit and put the whole business behind him. But he knew that it couldn't be done. He knew that as soon as he started to sell of his shares in large quantities, the price of coffee would plummet, and he risked taking a heavy loss.

A few times, he actually considered taking the risk. Even if the price would fall and he recovered only half the money he had invested, he would still be well off, even rich. What was the price of anxiety? Maybe it was best just to cut his losses and write off the whole coffee deal. But he found this a hard option to consider. It would be an admission of failure before the entire Portuguese community, a humiliation he could not endure. And besides, he told himself, he had a responsibility to Zuzarte, who had invested his small savings with him.

One morning, he decided to visit Amos Strasbourg in his office instead of going to the Exchange. He needed to talk.

"Well, look who's here," Amos greeted him. "I haven't seen you in at least a week. I was wondering where you were. Were you hiding from your pursuers? I was worried."

"If you wondered where I was, why didn't you come looking for me?"

Amos looked uncomfortable. "I didn't want to infringe on your privacy."

"Are we friends, Amos?"

Amos nodded gravely. "I hope so."

"Well, you don't worry about privacy if you're worried about your friend."

"All right. I accept the criticism. What's on your mind, Sebastian? What are you involved in these days?"

"Coffee and marriage."

"In that order?"

"Not necessarily."

"Do you want to explain?"

"Yes, I do," said Sebastian. "And I want to hear what you have to say. I don't know what to make of it. Do you know anything about coffee?"

"Not much. Only that it is a medicine and that it has a bitter taste. Oh, and that it comes from somewhere in Asia."

"That's something, I suppose. But first things first. You know Diego Zuzarte, the one who told us about the sugar hoax, the one who saved me from being run over a little while ago?"

"Of course. What about him?"

"He's been looking into coffee as an investment. He brought some coffee to the house, and my mother and I tried it. My mother called it bitter mud, which is a good description. But by the end of the evening, we couldn't get enough of it."

Amos sat up a little straighter. "Interesting," he said.

"More than interesting. Downright amazing. It made me feel as if all my senses were sharpened and that my mind was crystal clear like a mountain stream. You know something? My mind was racing so fast that I found it a little hard to fall asleep at night. I think I should drink coffee only in the morning or when I am fatigued and need to stay awake and alert."

"You've made me curious. I would like to try some myself."

"Come over to the house, and I'll make you some."

"Fine. Well, continue."

"So Zuzarte discovered this bean, and the Turk who gave it to him told him that coffee would soon become more popular in Europe than tea."

"Really, I find that hard to believe."

"I don't," said Sebastian. "And you won't either after you try it. Anyway, there's a ship call *Java Moon* coming in from the East Indies. Shares were available, and Zuzarte and I invested."

"Zuzarte invested? I though he was a broker."

"He put in a thousand guilders of his own money. He is really counting on this investment to make his fortune. And I'm also counting on it very much. Well, after we invested in the coffee shares a broker named Coronal put a large block of coffee shares on sale for a cheap price. Coronal refused to divulge the name of his client, and he said that his client refused to hold off for a few weeks, even though he could profit handsomely by doing so. We were forced to buy his shares to keep the price of coffee from collapsing."

"And you still have no idea who this client is?"

"None. Zuzarte thinks it may be Johannes Hoogaboom. But his suspicion is based on nothing substantial. Why would someone do that? Why would he try to drive down the price of coffee?"

"Perhaps he wants to hurt you," said Amos. "Perhaps this mysterious client is the same person who is behind the attacks and the betrayals. He is trying to destroy you. If he has not been successful in harming you physically, at least he intends to stop you from making a large profit."

"I'm really confused," said Sebastian. "Let's assume that there is one person behind all the things that have been happening to me and my family."

Amos nodded. "I think that is a fair assumption until we know otherwise."

"I cannot get a clear picture of this person. There are so many contradictions about this mysterious client. He betrays me in Vienna and tries to deliver me into the hands of the Inquisition, which means that he wants me dead. But then he doesn't kill me in the Black Forest when he has the chance; he just tries to steal my safe passage from the King of Poland. Then he tries to get my mother convicted of witchcraft, which would have meant a death sentence. But then he has his henchmen trap me in the alleyway in Amsterdam, but they don't kill me, even though they could have; they just try to steal my money. Then he has someone almost run me down on the Jodenbreestraat, which could easily have killed me if Zuzarte hadn't pushed me out of the way. So does he want to kill us or doesn't he?"

"I don't know. It is really baffling. And now, unless this business with Coronal is a pure coincidence, he is trying to prevent you from making a handsome profit. You know something ... Nah, it is probably not connected."

"What is it, Amos? Maybe it's important."

"All right, you be the judge. A little more than a week ago, maybe two weeks, I met Yakob Santos, one of the *parnassim* on your Maamad. He told me that he's seen you consorting with Zuzarte and that according to his sources Zuzarte is an unscrupulous man."

Sebastian slapped his hand on the table. "Don't you see what's happening? That was just about the time I was considering taking a position in coffee. So this mysterious client tries to undermine my confidence in Zuzarte and steer me away from him so that I would not make the investment. Once I made the investment, he tries to collapse the coffee market so that I should take heavy losses. He sends me the message through you, because he thinks you will immediately warn me. But you didn't. Why didn't you tell me about it?"

"Because I put no stock in it," said Amos. "Zuzarte strikes me as a fine young man. He saved us from that fake hurricane in Jamaica, and he saved your life. By the way, did he really save your life? Would you have been hurt by that wagon?"

"Amos, my good friend, the wagon missed me by little more than a hair. If Zuzarte hadn't pushed me down, the wagon would have run right over me. I don't know if it would have killed me but it certainly would have injured me badly. There is no question about it."

"No, I didn't think there was. So what was the point of running to you with idle rumors? I guess I disappointed the mysterious client. Once you invested in coffee, he had to buy up some shares and then sell them cheap. He probably would have collapsed the market if you hadn't bought them."

"Wait a minute," said Sebastian. "Did you say that Yakob Santos was the one who spoke to you against Zuzarte?"

"Yes. It was Santos."

"Do you think he's mixed up in this business? Do you think he might be the mysterious client?"

"I find it hard to believe," said Amos. "Why would he want to harm you?"

"Why would anyone want to harm me? What have I done to anyone?"

Amos shrugged. "I have no idea. Who would stand to gain by your loss?"

"I can't think of anyone."

"Certainly not Santos. Someone probably put him up to it. I'm sure he doesn't even realize that he was manipulated into speaking against Zuzarte. This enemy of yours is clever. Diabolically clever. He can probably get people to do his bidding without revealing himself to them."

"How about Karl and Steen?" said Sebastian. "Do you think they know his identity? I mean, we can peel away layer after layer of protection, but eventually someone has to know who he is."

"Not necessarily. He can meet with one or two agents in disguise and give them instructions and large sums of money. Then he can just sit back and observe the results, and no one knows who he is."

Sebastian stroked his chin thoughtfully. "You know, I think you're right. I don't think anyone knows who he is. This is so frightening. More than ever, I feel that we're up against a phantom, an evil wind that roars in, wreaks its havoc and vanishes into thin air."

"Have faith, Sebastian. The Almighty will not abandon you."

"I have faith, but I'm worried. Does that mean that I have no faith?"

"My dear friend, the Almighty does not demand such a high level of faith from you, at least not right away. As long as you believe completely that the Almighty is watching over you and guiding your steps, you are a true man of faith. Even if you are a little nervous. But enough of this morbid conversation. Let's talk about good things. Your brother Felipe is getting married soon, and I hear that you've become an uncle."

Sebastian beamed. "That's right. My sister Carolina has given birth to a boy. He is named Akiva, after my father. My mother may get married soon. And even I may soon marry."

"Really? Well, congratulations."

"Congratulations are a little premature, but it looks promising … Well, I'm glad I stopped by. I'll be going now. And don't forget to come by for a bowl of coffee."

"I won't forget," said Amos. "And take care of that investment. Be vigilant. Don't let the mysterious client get the best of you."

Sebastian passed the Exchange on the way back from visiting Amos. As it was still a good few minutes short of two o'clock, he decided to stop in and see if Zuzarte was there.

Zuzarte was indeed there, and he was extremely busy. Sebastian waited for the closing bell rang before he approached the broker.

"So what was all that about, Diego?" he asked. "More customers for coffee?"

"Not yet, senhor," said Zuzarte. "All is quiet on the coffee front, which is a good thing. But I have to keep working until the ship comes in, so I'm selling dried bananas."

"But I thought you don't believe in dried bananas."

"I don't believe dried bananas will be a big thing, like coffee. I wouldn't suggest it to you. But it's a commodity, and there's a customer for everything, especially if the price is right. The price has come down somewhat, and the people who are buying dried bananas are going into it with their eyes wide open. They'll make something, I'm sure, but we should save our money for coffee."

"Yes, we should," said Sebastian. "I wanted to talk to you about our coffee investment."

"Sure, talk."

"We have to protect the investment, which means we have to make sure the price doesn't drop suddenly."

"You're telling me! But the Coronal crisis is over. It's been quiet lately."

"And what if it happens again?" said Sebastian. "I believe it was done deliberately to hurt me."

Zuzarte's eyes widened. "But why?"

"I don't know. But I suspect it may happen again."

"So what should we do if it happens again? Are you willing to buy up everything that comes on the market?"

"I may just have to," said Sebastian.

"And what if it happens on an Exchange in a different city?"

"I didn't think of that," said Sebastian. "What do you suggest?"

"You can send standing instructions to agents in Hamburg, Paris, Madrid and Vienna to buy if a large block of coffee shares comes on the market. It can be arranged right away."

"Then that's what we'll have to do."

"Are you sure?" said Zuzarte.

"Yes, I'm sure. We have to defend the price of coffee."

"But you won't even know how much coffee is going on the market in these foreign cities, if it happens, Heaven forbid. You will have to open a line of credit and borrow the money if need be. I doubt you will have trouble obtaining a line of credit, but are you sure you want to do it? Maybe we should just forget about the whole venture. We can sell what we have, take our losses and then we can sleep peacefully."

"Is that what you want to do?" said Sebastian.

"No, of course not. But the main risk is not mine. It's yours. The most I can lose is my thousand guilders and my commissions. But you are really putting yourself at risk. Are you sure you want to do it?"

"I'm not sure," said Sebastian. "But let's do it anyway."

# THE NIGHT STALKER · 11

T HE ENGAGEMENT OF SEBASTIAN DOMINGUEZ and Dulce Castillo right after the festival of Sukkos caused a sensation in all of Amsterdam. The Dominguez family had been welcomed into the inner circles of the community by virtue of their illustrious lineage and their fame. But now that they had formed alliances by marriage with not one but two of the Naçao's most prominent families — the Pintos and the Castillos — they were perched on the very pinnacle of Portuguese society.

Meanwhile, preparations were going forward in the Dominguez home for Felipe's wedding, which was just six weeks away. Doña Angelica had her hands full with two impending marriages, and she was happy. As for her own future, she was slowly moving in a positive direction. Sergio Setubal had not yet made a formal proposal, but there was no question about his intentions.

"Senhora Dominguez," Eduardo Colon said to her one day, "we have to bring this matter to a conclusion. I understand that a match between older people is different from a match between youngsters. Older people have so many things and responsibilities on their minds that they simply cannot be rushed. But there is a limit, you know."

"I'm really sorry, Senhor Colon," said Doña Angelica, "but —"

"Sorry doesn't help, senhora. Forgive me if I speak a little strongly. You and Senhor Setubal have met several times, and each time, he signaled his willingness to meet again days before you did. Do you think he'll wait for you forever? Do you think there will always be other Sergio Setubals available for you?"

"Senhor Colon, I know full well how worthy Senhor Setubal is. He is a fine man, kind, warm and intelligent, and I really could not expect to find a husband like that so easily. Or a stepfather for my children and grandchild. But right now, I have two sons getting married, and it is too much for my mind and heart to absorb. It would mean a lot to me if you'd ask Senhor Setubal, in my name, to be a little more patient with me. I hold him in the highest regard, and it would be an injustice to him, and to me, if we were to consider a union without giving it our full and serious attention. Right now, I'm incapable of doing that. Please convey my apologies and assure him that he has no obligations to me."

Colon threw back his head and laughed. "You have said exactly what Senhor Setubal said you would say, senhora. Almost word for word. He told me to tell you that he understands perfectly and that he respects you for it. He also told me to convey to you that you may call on him for any service or assistance during this rather tumultuous period in your life. It will be his honor and privilege to assist you in any way he can."

After Colon left, Doña Angelica sat down on the divan and allowed herself a long sigh of relief. Then she went to see if Helga had followed her instructions for dinner. While in the kitchen, she brewed a pot of coffee and drank a full cup, savoring every drop of the bitter liquid.

Dinner was pleasant and leisurely. Afterward, Doña Angelica and Sebastian chatted for a while over tea, but Felipe had to return immediately to the *beis midrash*. He had arranged to have a special learning session with Rabbi Sasportas in his home. The old rabbi had rearranged his schedule specifically to learn with him, and Felipe did not want to keep him waiting, not even for a moment.

The streets of Amsterdam were illuminated by thousands of whale-oil lamps, which made its streets among the best lit in all of Europe. But the shadows of the gathering dusk still encroached between the islands of yellow light around the street lamps. As Felipe walked the mostly deserted streets, he was struck by a feeling that he was being followed. It was not something he heard or saw, just an intuition that an evil presence was there, lurking in the shadows. He spun around to look behind him, but he saw no one. As he walked on, he kept glancing over his shoulder to see if he could catch a glimpse of a flash of cloth or anything else that might give him a clue to the identity or whereabouts of the unseen stalker.

He crossed a footbridge over a small canal and immediately turned into a residential street on his right. He ran up the front stoop and positioned himself in the dark corner of the front doorway. Concealed from the street by the shadows of the overhang, he had a good view of the footbridge.

The waters below the footbridge glowed red in the light of the setting sun, but no one came across it. Felipe shook his head as if to clear it. Could he have been mistaken? He had been so sure that someone was following him, surer than if he had actually heard footsteps, but now he was not so sure any more. Perhaps it had all been a figment of his imagination.

He was about to step out of his shadowy hiding place when he heard a thud. He looked up and saw a man stagger across the footbridge, reeling drunkenly from side to side. The man stopped when he crossed the footbridge and leaned on a lamppost for support. Felipe could see him clearly from his vantage point. He was a big lumbering fellow in a sailor's pea coat and a woolen cap perched on top of a thick shock of sandy hair. The man looked both ways, muttering to himself. Then he turned to the left, the opposite direction from the one Felipe had taken, and rambled away.

Felipe waited until the sound of the sailor's receding footsteps faded away before he came out of his hiding place into the deserted street. His worries, he decided, were unfounded. The faint sounds of the sailor's footsteps had probably nudged the edge of his consciousness, although he was not aware of hearing anything. That explained the feeling of being followed when it was really nothing more than a drunken sailor trying to find his mates.

Nervous that he would now be late, he squared his shoulders and headed for Rabbi Sasportas' house, determined not to let his imagination get the better of him again. He thrust his hands into his pockets and turned his thoughts to a difficult ruling of the Rambam regarding certain of the laws of litigation that appeared in the Tractate Bava Kamma.

In his mind, he was transported to a *beis din* where two adversaries were presenting their conflicting arguments. One man demanded that the other one return the bushel of wheat he had given him for safekeeping. The other man denied ever having received a bushel of wheat for safekeeping, but he admitted that his adversary had given him a bushel of barley for safekeeping. Two issues presented themselves. One, considering that he had not denied the other man's claim completely, did he have to swear to validate his argument that he had received no wheat? Two, did his admission that he had received a bushel of barley obligate him to pay for it? Or did the other man's failure to ask for barley release him from this obligation?

Absorbed in his thoughts, Felipe did not hear the patter of the sailor's soft-soled footsteps coming up rapidly behind him. Despite his size, the sailor was as light as a cat on his feet. His collar was turned up, and the woolen cap was pulled down almost to his eyes, obscuring most of his face. There was no sign of his earlier drunkenness as he ran nimbly from one patch of shadow to the next, coming closer and closer to Felipe, who walked ahead, oblivious to the peril that loomed behind him.

The sailor pulled a dagger from his belt. He gripped the leather hilt in his meaty hand with the blade pointed forward, ready for a slash or an upward thrust. He braced himself and suddenly sprinted forward, his knife hand extended.

At the last moment, Felipe heard the approaching footsteps. But lost in his exploration of the Gemara, they did not register quickly in his mind.

"Watch out!" a voice shouted from behind him.

He spun around, and seeing the knife-wielding sailor bearing down on him, he turned and ran. The sailor glanced over his shoulder, and in an instant, he made an assessment of the situation. Three men were running toward him, shouting as they ran, and two of them were brandishing heavy canes. Doors were opening along the street as householders looked out to find the cause of the commotion. Felipe was already a distance away. There was no chance of catching him.

The sailor flipped the knife into the air and grabbed it by the blade. He cocked his arm and hurled the dagger toward the receding figure of Felipe. The dagger somersaulted through the air once, end over end. Then it flew straight as an arrow through a pool of lamplight that glinted off the metal of the blade and buried itself with a sickening thwack in Felipe's back. Felipe flung his arms outward and fell headlong to the ground.

As soon as the sailor saw the prostrate figure of Felipe with the knife protruding from his back, he fled down a dark alleyway. An instant later, the three men were at the opening of the alleyway into which the sailor had disappeared.

"What do we do, Senhor Sanchez?" asked one of the men, looking from Gonzalo to Felipe and back to Gonzalo.

"We go after him," said Gonzalo. "The people will take care of Felipe. Roelof, you go to the left. Piet, to the right. I'll go down the middle. Keep him penned in. All right, let's go."

The three men set off on their appointed routes at an easy lope. They knew the sailor would be conserving his energy and not running full tilt. At this point, strategy was more important than speed.

As Gonzalo had predicted, a few householders, who had been drawn from their homes by the commotion and witnessed the attack, ran to Felipe. A physician was immediately summoned, and no one touched the fallen young man until the physician came and directed that Felipe be carried into the nearest house.

Several blocks away, Roelof was the first to catch sight of the fleeing sailor. He was headed out of the Jewish quarter and into the Plantage. Roelof gave chase, staying to the left of the quarry and driving him toward the right. At the same time, Piet came barreling down the right side, forcing the quarry toward the middle, straight into the arms of Gonzalo. The sailor tried to break away from Gonzalo's grasp, but he was no match for Gonzalo's superior strength. Gonzalo wrestled him to the ground and sat on his chest. His legs folded under him pinned the sailor's arms.

Gonzalo peered down at the sailor's face, but he could not see him clearly in the fading daylight.

"Roelof, Piet," he shouted. "Knock on any door. Get us some lanterns. Now!"

The men ran off to get the lanterns, and Gonzalo looked down again at the captured sailor. He could not see his features clearly, but he could feel his fury.

"What's your name?" said Gonzalo.

The sailor responded by spitting at Gonzalo.

"That is not smart," said Gonzalo. He opened his hand

and slapped the sailor so hard that he cried out in pain. "Do that again, and I will hit you with my closed fist. I'll break your jaw. If you think this hurt, wait till I break your jaw. Now, we'll start again. What's your name?"

The sailor clamped his mouth shut and said nothing.

Roelof and Piet returned with three glass lanterns in which thick wicks burned in reservoirs of whale oil.

"Hold one of those over this rogue's face," said Gonzalo.

Roelof held the lamp aloft, and the sailor's face glowed amber. Gonzalo pulled off the sailor's woolen cap. There was no scar on his scalp. In fact, the scalp was covered by a thick growth of sandy hair. Just to make sure, he grabbed a clump of the sailor's hair and yanked hard. Clearly, the hair was real and not a wig. This was not Karl, Gonzalo decided. It was probably Steen, the other man who had attacked Sebastian in the alleyway off the Jodenbreestraat.

"What do you want to do with him, senhor?" asked Roelof. "Should we take him to the police? Or should we shoot him right here?"

"No, don't shoot him," said Gonzalo. "He has information that we need. When we're finished with him, we'll give him to the police. I mean, he's a criminal. He belongs in the custody of the police. But first, we should invite him to The Toothless Beggar for a brief visit. We can take him down to the cellar and have a productive conversation." Gonzalo stood up. "Grab hold of him, boys."

Roelof reached down and grabbed one of the sailor's arms and Piet grabbed the other, but they couldn't lift him up. The sailor made himself heavy as a lump and refused to move.

"Help me!" he shouted. "Someone call the police! I'm being attacked!"

Roelof and Piet were taken aback by this unexpected reaction. They dropped the sailor's arms and looked to Gonzalo for direction. The sailor took advantage of that moment of indecision. He leaped to his feet and bolted down the street.

The sailor was a big man, but he was fast. He ran past the main cluster of homes and out into the fields. Gonzalo and his men spread out and ran after him, but they were carrying their lanterns and could not run with full abandon. Gonzalo was about to tell them to douse their lanterns and run in the dark when he heard the sailor stumble and cry out in pain somewhere up ahead.

"He's hurt," said Gonzalo. "Let's go get him, but be careful. He may have more weapons. We should have searched him more carefully."

They were on a gravel path among a patchwork of vegetable gardens. The path led straight ahead to an old windmill whose sails were creaking noisily as they revolved in the early evening breeze. Behind the windmill was a canal.

"Roelof, give me your cane," said Gonzalo. Roelof handed Gonzalo his cane. It was identical to the one Piet was holding. "Good. Now, run ahead and get behind the windmill. He may make a run for the canal. Don't let him. Piet, check out the gardens to the left. I'll check the ones on the right side. And keep an eye on the path. If he gets past you and tries to get away, shoot him down."

Roelof went ahead and soon disappeared around the back of the windmill. Gonzalo and Piet walked slowly and deliberately into the shadowy gardens. They held their lanterns in front of them and probed at the vegetation with their canes.

"Steen!" shouted Gonzalo. "Do you hear me?"

There was no response.

"I know you're there, Steen. Come out, and we'll talk."

No response.

Gonzalo and Piet were moving forward. A few thickly overgrown vegetable gardens separated them from the windmill. The dense growth would make good camouflage for a man in hiding.

"Steen, we're coming closer!" shouted Gonzalo. "Listen to me. You're finished. We've got you surrounded. You can't get away. You're going to spend a long time in prison unless you end up on the gallows. Tell us what we want to know, and we'll put in a good word for you with the police."

There was still no response, other than ducks quacking on the pond.

"Steen! This is your last chance. If we have to struggle with you, I'll make sure that you swing from a rope."

The door to the windmill opened a crack, and the muzzle of a pistol crept out.

"Stay back," shouted Steen, "or I'll shoot."

"All right, Steen," said Gonzalo. "Just stay calm. Let's talk."

"What do you want?" said Steen.

"I want to know who put you up to this? Who's your employer?"

"I don't know."

"Where's Karl?"

"I don't know."

"Did Karl send you to kill Felipe Dominguez?"

"I don't know any Felipe Dominguez."

"Did you throw a knife at a young man tonight?"

"It's getting dark outside. It's hard to tell."

"Where does Karl live?"

"I don't know."

"Did you attack Sebastian Dominguez in an alley off the Jodenbreestraat a few months ago?"

"I don't remember what happened a few months ago."

"Is your name Steen?"

"Yes."

"What's your last name?"

There was a brief hesitation. "Schmidt."

"Are you sure that's your real name?"

"Yes."

"What's Karl's last name?"

"I don't know."

"Steen, Steen, you're not being helpful. You may have killed a young man just fifteen minutes ago. Don't you realize you are in deep trouble? Do you think I'll put in a good word for you just because you admitted to me that your name is Steen? That's worthless information, and besides, I knew that anyway."

"I don't know anything else."

"Steen, Steen, you're trapped inside that windmill. You're surrounded by three heavily armed men. Don't fool yourself. You won't get ten paces down the path before you'll have a bellyful of lead. If you don't cooperate, I'll send one of my men to call the police, and then the game will be over. It'll be straight to the gallows with you."

"So what will it be, Steen? The information or your life?"

There was no response.

"I asked you a question, Steen. The information or your life?"

"I'm thinking. I'm thinking."

"Well, think a little faster," said Gonzalo. "I'm getting tired of this."

"This is what I'm thinking. I'll put down my pistol, and you do the same with yours. Then you come into the windmill. We'll talk face to face. No weapons."

Gonzalo had no illusions about Steen's intentions, but he was prepared for treachery. He tucked one of his pistols into his belt behind his back where he could reach it easily should he need it. He also had a dagger strapped to his ankle.

"All right, Steen," he called out. "I'll put down my pistol if you toss out yours."

"Yours first," came the answer from behind the windmill door.

Gonzalo placed his pistol on the ground and kicked it forward.

"Good," said Steen. "Now walk forward and open your doublet. I want to see if you have another pistol in your belt."

Gonzalo opened his doublet. There was only a dagger in his belt.

"The dagger, too," said Steen. "And the cane."

Gonzalo dropped the dagger and the cane and kicked them forward.

"All right," said Steen. "Come in, holding the lantern in front of you."

The door opened a little wider to allow Gonzalo to enter. Behind the door, there was only gloom and shadows. The last fading light of the day did not penetrate inside the windowless windmill. Gonzalo held the lantern in front of him and walked through the door.

The stench of dry, rotted timbers immediately assailed his nostrils. He put his hand reflexively to his nose while he raised the lantern. The inside of the windmill was cramped by the ponderous grinding machinery powered by the wind-driven sails and by the stacks of dried wheat waiting to be ground. Steen was leaning against a post. One of his legs was lifted off the ground, as if it would be too painful to put his foot down, a sure sign of an ankle or knee injury.

Steen pointed to a hook on a post near the grinder. The wind had picked up, and the grinder was pounding up and down, up and down.

"Hang the lantern there," he said.

Gonzalo hung the lantern on the hook and turned to face Steen. A pistol had suddenly appeared in Steen's hand.

"Lock the door," said Steen, "and put the bolt in the brackets."

Gonzalo looked the door and placed the bolt across it.

"Put your hands on top of your head," said Steen.

"If you harm me," said Gonzalo, "my men outside will slit your throat."

"I know what I'm doing. Turn around. Slowly. And back toward me." Gonzalo backed up until he felt the muzzle of Steen's pistol probing the small of his back. Steen's other hand patted Gonzalo's lower back until he touched the concealed pistol.

"I'm not surprised," said Steen as pulled the pistol from Gonzalo's belt and tossed it onto a pile of grain sacks. "Now you listen carefully, my friend. I'm going to walk out of here with you as my hostage. My pistol will be planted in your back all the time. We passed a stable on the way here. You will tell one of your men to bring me a horse. The other man will stay where I can see him. If there is a false move, if someone tries to attack me or shoot me, I will have enough time to put a bullet in your back. It may not kill you, but you will never walk again. Do you understand me?"

"I understand you," said Gonzalo.

"All right. Let's go."

Steen reached up and put his left arm around Gonzalo's neck from behind. Gonzalo instantly spun toward his left, grabbed Steen's arm and flung him to the ground. Steen rolled over twice and came up with the pistol in his hand, but Gonzalo had already pulled the dagger from its ankle sheath. He slashed at the knuckles on Steen's right hand before he could squeeze the trigger. Steen dropped the pistol and howled in pain. Blood poured from the wound and covered his hand.

Crazed with pain and rage, Steen flung himself at Gonzalo and knocked the dagger from his hand. He pummeled at Gonzalo, but in the close quarters of their struggle, he could not land any solid punches. Screaming, he rolled away, grabbed a sack of wheat and hurled it at Gonzalo's head. Gonzalo ducked, but the sack struck him in the chest and knocked him on his back.

Disregarding the pain shooting up his injured leg, Steen grabbed a loose piece of timber and raised it high over his head, but before he could bring it down with full force, Gonzalo lifted his feet and kicked out at Steen's abdomen. Steen staggered back toward the grinder. He flung out his hand to regain his balance, but in the same motion, his hand knocked over the lantern.

As the lantern fell to the ground, its glass shattered and a stream of burning whale oil snaked into a pile of grain sacks. The fire licked at the tinder-dry grain, and it burst into flames with a loud whoosh. The flames leaped onto the dry, rotted timber of the wall, and in moments, one side of the windmill was ablaze. The heat sucked out the air and set the sails spinning even faster.

Gonzalo knew that in minutes not much more than charred residue would be left from the rotted old windmill and everything and everyone in it. He had to get out right away, but Steen stood between him and the door. He brandished the loose timber in his hand. Small flames were licking at its end as he moved warily toward Gonzalo with a look of madness in his eyes. Steen knew he would not survive this night, but he was determined to take Gonzalo with him.

The fire spread to the other walls and the roof of the windmill. The roar of the fire and the staccato pounding of the grinder were deafening in the small confined space of the interior of the windmill, but Gonzalo could hear another sound. It was the sound of fists hammering on the door. He thought he heard his name shouted, but he was not sure. Roelof and Piet were trying to break down the door, but the lock and the bolt were offering stiff resistance.

Gonzalo eyes smarted from the thick black smoke, and he felt that he couldn't breathe. In desperation, he looked around for something he could use as a weapon against Steen, and it was then that he caught sight of his pistol, the one Steen had found and tossed away. The pistol lay on a pile of grain that was already smoldering at the edges. At any moment, flames would engulf the sack and destroy the pistol.

Gonzalo lunged for the pistol, and Steen swung his piece of timber at Gonzalo's outstretched hand. Gonzalo pulled back his hand. The smoldering piece of timber swept through the spot vacated by Gonzalo's hand and struck the burning wall behind it. The force of the blow shook the wall, tore loose a flaming beam and sent it crashing down toward Steen.

Steen saw the beam falling in a fiery curtain of sparks. He raised his arms to protect his head, but the force of the beam sent him reeling backward toward the grinder. Steen heard the pounding of the grinder before he saw or felt it. He tried to arrest his fall, but his momentum carried his leg into the grinder. He screamed as if his lungs would tear apart, and his eyes rolled into his head.

Gonzalo ran to the door and tugged at the bolt, but he instantly pulled his hand back. The bolt was too hot to touch. He stepped back and aimed a kick at the underside of the bolt. The kick found its mark, and the bolt came loose and fell to the ground.

He pulled open the door and was greeted by a rush of cool, clean air. He filled his lungs and turned to look at Steen. The man lay on the ground. His crushed and mangled leg was covered with blood.

Steen's eyes pleaded with him.

"Help me!" he croaked. "I'll tell you everything I know."

Two more flaming beams crashed down on the fallen man.

"It's too late, my friend," Gonzalo said, and he stepped out into the open just as the entire windmill erupted into a huge, blazing inferno.

# LEMON CHEESE STRUDEL · 12

WHEN RABBI MORDECHAI STRASBOURG answered the knock on the door, the parrot was still perched on his shoulder, but the playful mischief in his eyes was replaced by a grave sadness. He stood aside as Sebastian, Amos and Gonzalo filed past, then he led them into his study.

"Before we discuss anything else, Sebastian," said the rabbi, "please give us the latest report on your brother's condition."

"Felipe is a strong fellow," said Sebastian. "He is holding his own. The knife struck his shoulder. The physicians say it did not damage any major organs, but there was a lot of bleeding. He is weak, but improving. He is getting excellent care. In the meantime, he is in Rabbi Sasportas's house until the physicians say he can be moved back home. My mother is there with him most of the time. She changes the dressings herself every few hours. We are grateful that he is alive. If Gonzalo and his men hadn't sounded the alarm, I … I don't even want to say what would have happened. It is too dreadful to consider."

"I understand," said the rabbi. "We all thank the Almighty that he is alive. Gonzalo, how was it that the three of you were there on the scene?"

"Well, rabbi, Don Sebastian asked me to arrange for protection and surveillance for his family. I assigned two men to each member of the family, and two men to watch the house during the night when the family slept. Yesterday evening, Roelof and Piet were assigned to Felipe. They are professional trackers who can follow without making their presence known. When they saw the sailor acting suspiciously, Roelof ran to get me, while Piet kept him under surveillance. I was in a tavern not more than two blocks away. I have to admit we were caught a little off guard. We did not expect an attack right in the middle of the street."

"It doesn't matter now, Gonzalo," said the rabbi. "You caught the assassin. That was important. But as I understand it, you didn't get much information from him. Except for a possibly fictitious last name."

"I wouldn't say that, rabbi," said Gonzalo. "We did pick up some useful evidence. Here."

He took out something wrapped in paper. He pulled apart the fold to reveal a piece of pastry.

"This is evidence?" said the rabbi.

"We found it on the ground outside the windmill. It was still fresh, so it must have fallen from Steen's pocket. This is lemon cheese strudel."

"Lemon cheese strudel," the rabbi repeated.

"That's right. Lemon cheese strudel. It's a German pastry."

The rabbi stared at him blankly. "A German pastry," he repeated.

"That's right, rabbi," said Gonzalo. "I recognize this pastry, but I haven't seen it in years. So I thought this might give us a clue. Last night, I inquired from my sources, and I was told that this pastry is sold in only two bakeries in all of Amsterdam. So I've posted a stakeout at both of these bakeries and given them a description of Karl Maybe Schmidt."

"That's a clever plan, Gonzalo. I hope it yields results. Right now, we need to put our heads together and see what we can figure out. We cannot allow this phantom to keep playing his game unopposed. Thank the Almighty that Felipe is alive and will recover, but what happens next time he makes an attempt? Amos, you look as if you have something on your mind."

"Actually, I do," said Amos. "First of all, I want to consider the possibility that the attack on Felipe was a case of mistaken identity. We've had no attacks on Felipe until now, just on Sebastian. And one on Doña Angelica, you know, the pressure to have a witchcraft trial. Is it possible that the attacker thought he was following Sebastian?"

Sebastian shook his head. "It's not likely. There is a certain family resemblance, and we have a similar build. But Felipe would never wear the kind of clothes I wear. He'd consider them far too flamboyant. Felipe dresses like the rabbi he is going to be. Don't forget, Steen and I have crossed paths before. In the alleyway off the Jodenbreestraat. He knows what I look like, and he wouldn't mistake Felipe for me."

"All right, that thought has been laid to rest," said Amos. "So let me get to my main point. It seems to me that the enemy, whoever he is, knows a lot about what goes on in the Dominguez family. For instance, he knew that Sebastian was traveling incognito to Vienna, and he sent his people to betray him and have him sent back to Spain. How did he know that, Sebastian?"

"He could have heard about it somewhere. I really don't know."

"When did you decide to go to Vienna?"

"In Hamburg," said Sebastian. "At my sister's wedding."

"And at the time your family was living in Paris and then in Metz and planning to settle in Amsterdam. Is that correct?"

"Yes."

"So before your sister's wedding, there was no connection between your family and Hamburg. Is that correct?"

"Yes. We had no contact with Hamburg."

"Now, you told me once," said Amos, "that it was a last-minute, spur of the moment decision. You left from Hamburg and went straight to Vienna. A day after your arrival, the police came and arrested you. How long was it from the time you decided to go until you actually left?"

"A few days," said Sebastian.

"That means that the enemy had very little time to make his evil plan and set it into motion. He had to send men to Vienna either at the same time you went or even earlier, because getting the police to come takes more than five minutes. Was it someone who lives in Hamburg who did this? Not likely. Most probably, it was someone who came to Hamburg at the time of the wedding or else he sent his agents to follow your family to Hamburg and cause mischief when they saw the opportunity. Who came to Hamburg for the wedding?"

"Just my family," said Sebastian. "And Elisha Ringel, a friend of my father's from Poland."

"Are any of these people suspects?"

"Of course not."

"So that leaves us with an agent of the enemy who followed you to Hamburg and discovered you were going to Vienna." He looked around the room. "Is my reasoning correct?"

"It sounds good," said Rabbi Strasbourg. "But we must always keep an open mind for the unexpected. In the meantime, proceed."

"I want to know," said Amos, "how this agent knew that Sebastian was going to Vienna. Did you talk about it to many people, Sebastian?"

"No, I did not. But Elisha Ringel may have mentioned something to someone. Or maybe his son Tanchum."

"Are they discreet people?"

"Elisha Ringel is definitely discreet," said Sebastian. "I imagine he's trained Tanchum to be discreet, too."

"Exactly. But even if one of these two men inadvertently dropped a word about it to someone somewhere, how did the enemy's agent know the precise address where Sebastian was to be found in a village near Vienna?"

Amos looked around the room from face to face. No one had an answer.

"Let's go on," said Amos. "The men who attacked us in the Black Forest are not such a mystery. They were probably under orders to stay in Vienna until Sebastian was shipped off to Spain. After Sebastian was released, they followed him and waited for the opportunity to attack him on a deserted stretch of road. The push to bring Doña Angelica to trial is also not such a mystery. The enemy's agents following the family would learn about the witchcraft accusation without much difficulty. There was time and opportunity there for the enemy to organize pressure on the magistrate. But the attack in the alleyway off the Jodenbreestraat baffles me. What were Karl and Steen after, Sebastian?"

"They wanted the pouch I was carrying."

"Exactly," said Amos. "They didn't try to kill you, although they could have. We'll discuss that issue separately, but let's leave it for now. They wanted your pouch because they thought you had money in it. Were you carrying a lot of money that day, Sebastian?"

"Yes, I was. Letters of credit worth a hundred thousand guilders."

"A hundred thousand guilders!" said Amos. "Do you carry that much money around with you every day?"

Sebastian wanted to laugh but he could only manage a weak smile. "Not usually. In fact, never. Only on that day."

"Only on that day," Amos repeated slowly and deliberately, drawing out each syllable. "How did they know you would be carrying a lot of money — a king's ransom of money — on that very day? Was it a lucky guess? Does anyone want to venture a guess?"

There was silence for several long moments.

"It seems," said Rabbi Strasbourg, "that they had inside information. Someone with access to information about the family has been feeding them information. But who could it be?"

Gonzalo slapped his hand on the table. "It's obvious," he said. "Helga the Norwegian."

"Who's that?" said Rabbi Strasbourg.

"She's the housekeeper," said Gonzalo. "She's been with the family since Paris and Metz. She went with them to Hamburg. She must have overheard Don Sebastian telling his mother about his plans."

"But that's impossible," said Sebastian. "She's a simple woman, and she speaks nothing except Norwegian and terrible French. If I ever say anything to her in German or Spanish, it's like talking to the wall."

"Maybe she doesn't want you to know she understands," said Rabbi Strasbourg. "Maybe she's the invisible person, the fly on the wall that hears everything. Did you tell your mother you would be carrying money to the bank the next day, Sebastian?"

"I believe I did. No, I'm sure I did."

"So she hears you and slips away to tell the enemy's agents. And let's not forget that she was the one who reported your mother to her priest and caused the witchcraft accusation."

"But she didn't do it until weeks after the event," said Sebastian.

"It seems to me," said Rabbi Strasbourg, "that she reported immediately to the agents, and then she waited for further instructions. The enemy chose the time to set the accusation into motion."

"But why would she do such a thing?" said Sebastian.

"Money," offered Gonzalo. "They probably approached her in Paris and offered her money. She was the perfect spy inside the household. It was as if they had some kind of machine inside your house that allowed them to eavesdrop on everything that was going on."

"I admit that there is a logic to what you're saying," said Sebastian. "And I certainly don't want to be her defender. She is not a very likable person. But I find it hard to believe she understood our conversations. She never shows the least bit of interest in what we are saying, and she only responds when we speak to her in French."

"We'll soon find out," said Gonzalo. "From here, we'll go straight to your house and have a talk with Helga the Norwegian."

"Wait a minute, Gonzalo," said Rabbi Strasbourg. "You're saying that she really understands German and Spanish, but she kept it a secret from the family."

"That's right."

"And then the enemy approached her and offered her money to spy for him."

"That's right."

"So tell me, why did she make believe she didn't know German and Spanish? Wouldn't Senhora Dominguez have been more eager to hire her had she revealed her knowledge of these languages?"

"I suppose so."

"And then the enemy got lucky and found a housekeeper in the Dominguez home who had a secret knowledge of German and Spanish and was willing to spy on the family for money. How very convenient."

Gonzalo scratched his head. "You're right, rabbi. I didn't think of that."

"Unless," said the rabbi, "the enemy planted her there in

the first place."

"Exactly!" said Gonzalo. "That's what must've happened. This is even more diabolical than I first thought."

"How horrible," said Sebastian. "I can't believe that my mother has been living with a snake in her home almost from the day she came to France. Helga works hard and keeps the house in shape, so my mother relies on her. She even took her along to Hamburg for my sister's wedding, because she is so dependent on her. And all this time, she's been stabbing us in the back." Hearing his own words, Sebastian grimaced with anger. "Poor Felipe. Poor all of us."

"Not for long, Don Sebastian," said Gonzalo. "Not for long. Let's go to your house. In a short while, we'll have some answers. There's no need for you to trouble yourself, rabbi. But Amos might want to come along."

"Amos will come," said the rabbi. "And so will I. It's no trouble."

Twenty minutes later, the four men were sitting in the parlor of the Dominguez house. Doña Angelica was in Rabbi Sasportas's house taking care of Felipe. Helga was in the kitchen cutting vegetables.

"Helga, please come here," Sebastian called out in French.

There was a clatter of utensils in the kitchen, and Helga emerged, wiping her hands on her apron as she passed through the central hall.

Gonzalo was standing near the staircase.

"*No se mueva, señora*," he said in an even tone as she passed. "*Usted está en peligro.*" (Don't move, he was saying. You are in danger.)

Helga froze and turned to stare at Gonzalo.

"*Vorsichtig,*" he added. "*Eine Schlange auf Ihrem Fus Ist.*" (Careful, there is a snake on your foot.)

Helga shrieked in terror and sprang back. She looked

down at first one foot and then the other, and she saw that there was no snake. Realization appeared in her eyes, and then fear. She turned to run, but Gonzalo blocked her way.

"Listen carefully, you repulsive witch," he said in rapid Spanish. "You're in deep trouble. I'll be calling the police soon, and you'll be arrested. That cannot be avoided. You've committed many serious crimes, and you're an accessory to many others. You will pay for your crimes and your treachery, but the question is how much you'll pay. Your head will roll — and the world will be better off without scum like you — unless you tell us everything you know. We can prevail on the police to let your head remain attached to your neck, but you must give us your full cooperation. If I sense you're holding back, the conversation will be over, and the police will be summoned immediately. Do you understand?"

"Yes, I understand," she said.

"Sit down," said Gonzalo. "In the parlor. I want the other gentlemen to hear what you say. We will speak in German."

Helga went into the parlor and sat down. Unable to meet Sebastian's eyes, she looked down at her feet. While she waited for the interrogation to begin, she grabbed the ends of her apron and twisted them over and over again, and she bit her lower lip until it turned white.

"It wasn't my fault," she said when Gonzalo took his seat across from her. "Karl made me do it."

"Who is Karl?" asked Gonzalo. "And what power does he have over you?"

"Karl is my brother. He tells me what to do, and I have to do it. That's just how it is, ever since we were children."

"What is Karl's last name?"

"Schmidt."

"Who is Steen?"

"He's our cousin. Steen Schmidt. Karl and Steen are best friends."

"I see. Are you Norwegian?"

"No, we're German. From Stuttgart. A grandmother was Norwegian. That's why my name is Helga and I speak a few words of Norwegian."

"Tell us what happened."

"I was looking for work as a nurse in Antwerp," she said. "Karl wrote to me and told me to come to Paris immediately. One of his clients needed a job done. He said he had gotten me a job as a housekeeper for a Spanish lady. The pay was small, but his client would pay me handsomely in addition to my salary. All I had to do was give him certain information from time to time. So I did it." She turned to Sebastian. "I am so sorry, Senhor Dominguez. I didn't mean any harm. I didn't know that Karl intended to hurt you or your mother or Felipe. Please forgive me."

Sebastian looked at her with disdain and turned away.

"You'll make your apologies later," said Gonzalo. "Where is Karl? We already have a lot of the information from Steen, but we want you to confirm it independently."

"Steen didn't tell you anything," she said. "You could tear out his fingernails one by one, and still, he would tell you nothing to betray Karl."

"But you would?"

Helga flushed, and she looked down at her hands. "I'm not strong like Karl and Steen. I'm just a weak woman. I don't want to suffer."

"Tell us the truth, and your suffering will be reduced."

"Yes, yes," she said. "I will."

"All right," said Gonzalo. "Where is Karl?"

"I don't know. I swear I don't. When he wants to talk, he hangs a ribbon in the old elm tree across the street. I do the same when I want to talk to him. We both check it every day, morning and night. We meet at the Herrengracht."

"Who is Karl's client?"

"I don't know that either. And I don't think Karl knows. They meet somewhere in secret. The client does not reveal his identity. He just brings instructions and cash. A lot of cash. Karl always has plenty of money for his jobs, and there's plenty left over for his own pocket."

Gonzalo leaned back. He had run out of questions to ask.

"Apparently, you do not know as much as we expected," said Rabbi Strasbourg. "I'm curious. Does Karl like bread or pastries?"

"He likes hot fresh bread," said Helga. "Who doesn't? But he loves pastries, especially lemon cheese strudel. He buys it for himself and for Steen. Sometimes, he brings me some of it. Why do you ask?"

"We will ask the questions," said Gonzalo. "You just give us honest and complete answers."

"Did you know where he gets these pastries?" asked the rabbi. "There are numerous bakeries in Amsterdam. Do you know from which bakery he gets them?"

"No, he doesn't get them in a bakery," said Helga. "He buys it from a woman who sells it to bakeries. He saves money that way."

"Where does she live?" asked Gonzalo.

"I have no idea," said Helga, obviously pleased that she was unable to provide a clue to his whereabouts.

There was a loud knock at the door. The conversation stopped as Sebastian went to see who was there. A minute later, he returned.

"I have to go," he announced, "but you can stay here and continue what you were doing."

"Is everything all right?" asked the rabbi. "Is it about Felipe?"

"It's not about Felipe," said Sebastian. "It was a message from Johannes Hoogaboom at the Bank of Amsterdam. He says he wants me to come down immediately. You ask if everything is all right. I hope it is, but I won't know till I hear what he wants."

Sebastian walked to the bank in a red haze. He felt that his world was collapsing around him. His brother was lying wounded in someone else's house. As for his mother, instead of being involved with joyous preparations for her younger son's wedding, she was sitting by his bedside and changing his dressings. And he himself, what was he doing? Grasping at straws in the dark, trying to find a clue to the identity of his tormentor. And trying to stave off financial ruin.

How had he allowed himself to come to this point? No one had forced him to plunge so deeply into coffee. Zuzarte had offered him the opportunity with the best intentions. The man had saved him from taking a loss in the sugar market, and even more important, he had saved his life! If not for Zuzarte, the wagon would have run him over and crushed him. There was no doubt about it. So does a man save someone's life one day and cheat him the next?

Zuzarte was on his side, there could be no doubt. He had brought him the coffee deal, but Sebastian was the one who made the decision to invest. He had invested heavily but only with his own money. He had not gambled with other people's money. He had only taken a calculated risk with his own. And now he regretted the day he had put that first bowl of coffee to his lips.

But why had he done it? he asked himself. Why hadn't he stayed the course with his conservative investments and moderate profits? He didn't need the money. He had more than enough money to last him for years, and his conservative plan of investment was bringing him a respectable steady income. Why did he need the coffee venture? Why did he need the risks?

It was the glory, he decided. He wanted to do something

great in his own right, by his own talents and initiative. If he had made a fortune as a financial visionary who discovered a new and important market, he would have earned honor and respect in the community beyond anything he had ever experienced. It was not enough to be famous for having escaped from prison and the Inquisition. He wanted to be famous for something he had accomplished.

At this moment, however, Sebastian decided that he would gladly forfeit all fame and glory for a little security and peace of mind. The coffee venture had drawn him in to the point where he was extended to the limit. He was holding on by his fingernails, so to speak, hoping that *Java Moon* arrived with its boatload of coffee before his pockets were completely emptied.

Sebastian was ushered into Hoogaboom's office as soon as he arrived at the bank. Once again, his wife was sitting at her desk, but it was as if she were not there at all.

"Thank you for coming so promptly, Senhor Dominguez," said Hoogaboom. "First of all, let me offer my condolences to your family for the dreadful event of last night. We are all shocked and dismayed, and our prayers are with your brother and your entire family."

"That is very kind of you," said Sebastian.

The banker cleared his throat. "Unfortunately, business waits for no man. Even in times like these, when I would like nothing more than to allow you to deal with your tragedy undisturbed, I must fulfill my duties to the bank."

"I understand."

"I am aware of your recent activities in the market. The coffee market in particular. We spoke about it once before. Well, you have taken matters to a different level. I understand that you have to protect your investment. It is to be expected. But until now, you've been playing with your own money. Now you are playing with the bank's money. Your agents in

Paris, Hamburg and Madrid have purchased blocks of shares that have become available in those markets, and they've paid for their purchases with your line of credit at this bank."

"How much did they spend?"

"A substantial amount in total," said the banker. "You do not have enough money on deposit here to cover the credit we have extended to you."

Sebastian looked at Hoogaboom without saying a word.

"You have put us at risk," said Hoogaboom, "and banks do not like to be at risk. If you had been conducting business as you have in the past, the bank might be a little more patient with you. But your risky behavior of late has … somewhat … reduced our confidence in your ability to meet your obligations."

"I think I am a responsible trader," said Sebastian. "I have never failed to meet my obligations."

"That was true in the past. I am not so sure about the future. So the bank wants you to pay off the balance on your credit account within three days. We will allow you to maintain a credit line, but a substantially reduced one."

Sebastian took a deep breath. "I see," he said. "I suppose there would no point in asking you to reconsider."

"None."

"Then I have no choice. How much do you need?"

"Twenty-seven thousand three hundred guilders."

Sebastian was beside himself. "Twenty-seven thousand!"

"Yes. And three hundred."

"Can you give me a week?"

"Three days is generous, Senhor Dominguez. I cannot do better."

Sebastian had come to the bank in a haze, and he left in a daze. Twenty-seven thousand guilders! The most he could manage on his own was maybe twelve thousand, which would leave him penniless and still at least fifteen thousand guilders short. There was no choice. He needed to borrow money, and fast. Except for the credit line at the bank, he had never borrowed money in his life, and the thought of it mortified him.

According to the clock in the bank, it was still fifteen minutes shy of one o'clock. Sebastian decided to stop by the Exchange on the way home. Perhaps he would come up with an idea. There were a number of traders, some of them exceedingly wealthy, with whom he had excellent business relations. Perhaps he could persuade one or two of them to lend him some of the money he needed to cover his shortfall at the bank.

Yakob Santos and Martino Vega were deep in conversation with a third man in the corner occupied by the wheat traders. Sebastian had the impression that Yakob Santos had glanced at him and quickly turned away, but he was not sure. It could have been his overheated imagination.

"Good afternoon, Senhor Dominguez," said a voice at his elbow. It was Eduardo Colon, this time dressed in a light green outfit with black trim and feathers in his hat to match. "We are all so sorry to hear about your misfortune. Rabbi Sasportas has told me that Felipe is expected to recover. I tell you, no one is happier than the rabbi, and your family, of course. Felipe has become very dear to him. He would be devastated should anything happen to your brother. Our prayers are with you."

"They are much appreciated, Senhor Colon."

"Ahem, your young friend Diego Zuzarte is quite busy today," said Colon. "Is he doing your bidding?"

"I'm not sure I know what you mean."

"Have you just arrived?"

"Yes. Just minutes ago."

"Then you haven't heard?"

"Heard what?" said Sebastian.

"The latest rumor from the East Indies," said Colon. "There is a ship arriving a week or two after *Java Moon*. It is called *Sumatra Moon*. Among its cargoes, it is also carrying a substantial load of coffee."

The blood drained from Sebastian's face.

"You are right to be concerned, Senhor Dominguez. If this rumor is true, there will be too much coffee on the market. Who needs so much coffee anyway? According to what I hear, it's vile stuff not good for anything except for colds and fevers. I suppose there would be a market for a limited amount of the stuff, but two boatloads? Forgive me for speaking like this about a product in which you have invested, but I believe in being forthright and telling the truth."

"Of course," said Sebastian. "That is very commendable. But I must excuse myself. We can continue this chat another time."

After searching desperately among the crowds of traders scattered all over the trading floor, Sebastian finally managed to find Zuzarte.

Zuzarte took one look at his face and said, "You heard?"

"I heard."

"Don't panic," said Zuzarte. "It's only a rumor, and the source is not very reliable. Most traders are not giving the rumor much credence. But it is still a time of peril for us. If some of the traders holding coffee shares get jittery and try to sell off some of their shares, the price may start to drop. Then there's no telling what may happen. There may be a panicked sell-off, and the price will collapse."

"It seems we're always walking a tightrope," said Sebastian. "One wrong step and we fall to the ground."

"It feels that way sometimes, senhor. You need strong nerves for this business. The question is this. What do we do now?"

"Do you have suggestions?" said Sebastian.

"Actually, I do. You can't afford to buy up all the shares that may be dumped on the market, and I certainly can't. But we can get other people to do it. You can ask your friends here in the exchange to buy up shares for themselves so that the price will be stable. They'll make a nice profit once the ship comes in. And in the meantime, that's exactly what I've been doing. So far, I've convinced three people to buy the shares and support the price."

Sebastian considered this for a moment, then he nodded.

"Good work, Diego. And good thinking. Let me see what I can do."

For the next hour, Sebastian lobbied his friends and associates on the Exchange. He told them all about his experiences with coffee and how the people who try it become obsessed with its powers. There was no doubt that it would soon become a sensation in all of Europe. It was only a matter of time, Sebastian assured them. If only they'd agree to support the price against these eruptions of false rumors, there would be handsome profits for all of them in the end.

Sebastian's passionate arguments were persuasive, and a number of the people he approached — some Jewish and some not — promised to buy all shares that appeared on the market.

Sebastian was relieved. The participation of these prominent traders would not only keep the price from collapsing, it would actually drive it upward. But suddenly he realized that his other problem had become even more aggravated. All the traders on the Exchange from whom he thought he could borrow had now committed themselves to help him support the price of coffee on the market. He couldn't very well go back to them for loans.

He needed fifteen thousand guilders desperately.

And he had only three days to find the money.

# CLOAK AND DAGGER · 13

**E**ARLY THE NEXT MORNING, Gonzalo and Roelof stood chatting under a spreading elm half a block from the squat house at 23 Bruggenstraat. They faced each other as they chatted, each one keeping an eye on the street behind the other. A pony cart stood in front of the house. Gonzalo was sure it was there to pick up the pastries.

It had not been too difficult for Gonzalo's men to discover this address. The owners of the two bakeries had been reluctant to divulge the whereabouts of the culinary artist that provided them with the heavenly German pastries, but a little persuasion had changed their minds.

Gonzalo knew that if Karl came at all that day he would come before she sent off her pastries to the bakeries. That is, unless she had a standing order to leave a few for him every day. Gonzalo did not consider that likely.

A man in a leather coat, a woolen cap pulled low over his eyes, turned into the Bruggenstraat a block to the east of the house under surveillance. Roelof, who was facing east, described him to Gonzalo, who listened carefully without turning around. The man whistled a carefree tune as he walked. He stopped at the squat house and exchanged a few words of familiar greeting with the driver of the pony cart. Then he went into the house and emerged a minute later with a package.

He waved good-bye to the driver and headed back in the direction from which he had come. Gonzalo and Roelof followed at a discreet distance. The man stopped at a tobacconist's shop, but he didn't buy anything. He just stood there, looking around as if expecting someone. Presently, a street urchin came up to him, handed him a scrap of paper and trotted away. The man looked at the paper, then he crumpled it and tossed it away.

The man continued walking, with Gonzalo and Roelof trailing behind. Gonzalo made sure to scoop up the crumpled piece of paper as he passed the tobacconist's shop and thrust it into his pocket. The man entered a well-appointed rooming house for single men. After a few minutes, he had still not come out, which seemed to indicate that this was his place of residence. He had obviously come home to enjoy his morning strudel with his breakfast.

Gonzalo pulled the crumpled paper from his pocket and unfolded it. It read, "9 Kirche." Kirche was the German word for church. It seemed to be instructions for a rendezvous. Nine o'clock in the evening at an unspecified church. Gonzalo was convinced that the German-speaking unmarried man in the rooming house was Karl Schmidt, and that the man he was going to meet in the evening in a church somewhere was his employer. The end was coming closer, Gonzalo could feel it. The important part now was to follow Karl to his rendezvous without being spotted.

While he himself remained at his vantage point across from the rooming house, Gonzalo sent Roelof for reinforcements. He needed a team of at least five or six trackers to switch off regularly so that Karl wouldn't see the same person more than once or twice should he look back over his shoulder.

The trackers were posted inconspicuously all around the rooming house, but Karl did not come out for the rest of the day. It was dark when he finally appeared. He was wearing a long cloak that covered him from his shoulders to below his knees. He looked both ways, more out of habit than out of suspicion, and headed off into the night.

Karl did not take any circuitous routes or double back as he might have done had he suspected he was being followed. He walked through a neighborhood with several churches, but none of those was the meeting point. He turned into the Barroesstraat, a broad boulevard ablaze with lamplight and thronged with revelers. The trackers moved closer as Karl moved through the crowds and fell back when the crowds thinned. He approached the massive Oude Kerk, the oldest church in Amsterdam, but passed right by it. This too was obviously not the meeting place.

After walking north, Karl turned east and crossed a canal on a footbridge, then he walked for a very long distance and crossed another canal on a footbridge. He entered a quiet neighborhood in the extreme northeast of the city, very far from the Jewish quarter, and turned into one of the smaller streets. He stopped before a small but well-lit building.

A sign on the front door identified it as the Church of Saint Jerome. It was a Catholic church, an unusual sight in Amsterdam, where the Dutch Reformed Church was supreme. The Dutch allowed Jews to build large synagogues, but they would not allow the Catholic Church, their old nemesis, to build more than the most modest prayer houses. And this was one of them.

A tall man waited outside the church. He greeted Karl with a brief nod of his head, and they went into the church together. The man had an air of authority about him. He was wearing a long hooded cloak, as was Karl. The hood was pulled over the man's head, and his face was concealed from those watching from afar. But there was nothing to prevent Karl, who had faced him directly, from seeing his features.

Clearly, the man's identity was no secret from Karl.

*It makes sense,* thought Gonzalo, *that one person should know the phantom's identity.* That one person would be able to communicate at length with his employer and serve as the conduit for all his missions and instructions. For the phantom, this one person whom he had taken into his confidence was Karl. This made Karl doubly valuable. He had led them to the phantom, and he could give them important information if they could trap him and persuade him to talk.

Gonzalo assigned two of his men to follow Karl when he came out. Gonzalo, Roelof, Piet and two others would follow the phantom.

After the men were in position, Gonzalo went into the church. A priest greeted him in the vestibule.

"Vespers are over," he said. "But you can light a candle to your patron saint or just stay and pray if you wish. Are you a Catholic?"

"Yes, father, I am. Actually, I was looking for someone. Two gentlemen came in a few minutes ago. I wanted to have a word with the taller one. He is my brother-in-law."

"Ah, you mean Senhor Salazar. He is a fine gentleman. We do not get many people of his caliber here. Mostly, old women and a few laborers."

"My brother-in-law speaks highly of this church," said Gonzalo.

"That is very kind of him," said the priest. "He has been coming here for years. He is such a devout man. I enjoy watching him pray. And he always leaves a generous donation in the collection plate. Senhor Schmidt, however, is a bit of a roughneck, but Heaven loves all people, I always say. Anyway, feel free to go in and look for them."

Gonzalo looked into the sanctuary of church. It was a very small area, but it was set up with rows of pews and an altar in front of a cross. He could see Karl kneeling in a pew toward the back on the right side, but there was no sign of Senhor Salazar.

Gonzalo stepped back out into the vestibule. The priest was still there, puttering with a broken chair.

"Excuse me, father," said Gonzalo. "I see Senhor Schmidt, but I do not see my brother-in-law. Do you know where he might be?"

"He's probably gone," said the priest. "He often leaves by the back door. It opens into the next street. I'm surprised that Senhor Schmidt is still here. They usually leave together."

"I think I'll have a word with Senhor Schmidt," said Gonzalo. "But first I have to step outside for a moment."

The priest shrugged and went back to his puttering.

Gonzalo stepped into the street and signaled to Roelof. "Quick! Our man probably left by the back door. It opens into the next street. Send men around the cross streets on both sides. We may still have a chance. And tell them to be on the lookout for Karl in case he decides to go out the back way, too. Hurry!"

Roelof ran off, and Gonzalo ran back into the church. The priest gave him a queer look as he ran by him, but he just shrugged again and went about his business.

The sanctuary was almost completely in darkness. Two old women dressed in black were lighting candles near the altar, the glow of the candles sending their eerily distorted shadows onto the faint walls. Karl was still in the same position, kneeling in the pew in the back, his clasped hands in front of him, his forehead resting on his hands. He seemed to be deep in prayer.

Gonzalo walked over quietly. He put his right hand on the pistol in his belt, and with his left hand, he touched Karl lightly on the shoulder. There was no reaction. He shook Karl's shoulder a little harder.

Karl toppled over to the ground. His cloak fell away from

his left side to reveal the hilt of a dagger protruding from his back. The thrust must have penetrated directly to his heart, instantly stopping its pumping action, because there was not a great deal of blood. The body had been arranged to appear as if he was kneeling in prayer.

Gonzalo pulled the wool cap from Karl's head just to confirm the identification. The bald pate with its jagged scar was unmistakable. It was Karl.

Without touching the body, Gonzalo stepped out into the aisle and looked around. The two old women were still busy with their candles. Karl's body lay where it had fallen, covered by the shadows of the darkened pew.

Back on the street, Roelof was waiting for Gonzalo.

"The news is not good," he said. "He was long gone by the time the trackers came around to the back of the church. We searched the streets all around. There weren't too many people outside, but we asked whomever we saw. No one had anything useful for us. This time of the year, there are many tall men wearing long cloaks in Amsterdam. Did you have any luck with Karl?"

"Karl's dead," said Gonzalo. "A knife in the back."

"Oh."

"Exactly. Oh. Well, I'm going over to Rabbi Strasbourg's house. If you need me, you'll know where to find me."

It was close to eleven o'clock when the meeting in Rabbi Strasbourg's study convened. Sebastian looked pale and drawn as he listened to Gonzalo report the evening's events. Amos looked as if he was working hard to control his anger. But Rabbi Strasbourg was calm. His face remained impassive, and he listened with deep concentration. Hurdus slept in his cage with the door open.

"The question, of course," said Rabbi Strasbourg, "is why did the enemy — let's call him Salazar for want of a better name — why did this Salazar kill Karl?"

"I think it was fear," said Sebastian. "He was afraid we were getting too close to Karl. So he killed him to protect himself."

"Why would he suddenly think this?" said the rabbi.

"Well, we got to Steen," said Sebastian. "Maybe he thinks Steen talked."

"I don't think so," said Amos. "Salazar is clever and cunning. I'm sure that Steen never saw Salazar. After all, why should Salazar meet with him? Showing himself to Karl was more than enough. So Steen could not lead us to Salazar. At most, he could lead us to Karl. But Salazar surely knew that Steen would never betray Karl, just as Helga told us. And even if he did somehow lead us to Karl, we would have to get Karl to talk. I don't think he would have broken as quickly and as easily as Helga did. So Salazar was still well insulated, even though we got to Steen. So why should he suddenly decide to kill Karl?"

"I agree with Amos," said the rabbi. "But there is another question. It seems clear that Karl was the only one who ever saw Salazar, as Amos pointed out, because he was Salazar's primary agent for all his schemes. Are we all agreed?"

They all nodded.

"Karl was very important to Salazar. Agreed?"

They nodded again.

"So what is he going to do now? Where will he find another Karl?"

No one had an answer to the rabbi's question.

"I think he will not seek another Karl," said the rabbi. "I suspect that he is close to his end game. Whatever devious, diabolical plan this Salazar has in mind, I think he is almost there."

"You're saying that he killed Karl," said Sebastian, "because he doesn't need him anymore?"

"Exactly," said the rabbi. "Salazar is an unscrupulous

man. Now that he's close to his goal, Karl is only a liability. He doesn't need his henchman anymore. Karl can only be trouble for Salazar. So Salazar got rid of him."

"The man is a monster," said Amos.

"That is a fair statement," said the rabbi. "But we're not done here. What else do we know about this Senhor Salazar?"

"He is either Spanish or Portuguese," said Amos.

"How do you know that?" said the rabbi.

"Well, his name is Salazar. That wouldn't prove anything, because anyone can have an Iberian family name. But the priest identified him as Senhor Salazar. If he was Dutch the priest would have identified him as Mijnheer Salazar."

"Good point," said the rabbi. "What else do we know?"

"He is probably not Jewish," said Sebastian. "A Jew wouldn't arrange to meet in a church of all places."

"Yes, and Jews are usually not murderers." The rabbi looked over at Gonzalo. "Not that gentiles are necessarily murderers."

"It's true, rabbi," said Gonzalo. "A very small percentage of people can commit murder, and hardly any of them is ever a Jew. I agree with you that Salazar is not Jewish. My impression from the short conversation I had with the priest is that Salazar has been coming to the church for a very long time, that he prays and that he makes generous contributions to the collection plate. The man is a Catholic."

# THE LAST STRAW · 14

SALAZAR, THAT IS THE NAME OF MY ENEMY, thought Sebastian as he walked to the Exchange the next morning. He knew, of course, that Salazar was not his enemy's real name, but even so, it brought his enemy into a little more focus in his own mind. The man was tall, he attended a Catholic church in a remote corner of Amsterdam and he called himself Salazar. The phantom was beginning to have a form.

Sebastian's immediate concern, however, was his need to find fifteen thousand guilders and deliver the money to the bank by the next day when the three-day deadline would arrive. He was hoping that somehow an opportunity might present itself at the Exchange.

When he stepped onto the trading floor of the Exchange, he looked around and saw only the usual scenes of frenetic business activity which had become so familiar to him during the many months of his membership. He greeted his friends and associates and sidestepped the brokers, hoping against hope that something would happen to rescue him from his predicament.

He caught sight of Zuzarte at the same time Zuzarte caught sight of him. The broker immediately interrupted his conversation and came to greet him.

"Senhor Dominguez, wonderful news," he said, his face wreathed in smiles. "The rumor about the *Sumatra Moon* turns out to be nothing more than that, an insidious rumor. There is no such ship, nor is any other ship sailing toward Amsterdam with a load of coffee other than our own *Java Moon*."

"Well, that is a relief," said Sebastian.

"It is more than a relief. It is our promise of real riches. The price of coffee has not only stabilized, it has actually gone up a bit this morning. All those people who bought coffee the day before yesterday as a personal favor to you, to keep the price of coffee from collapsing, all those people have already made a tidy profit. I even heard that some of them were buying more shares of coffee now that the rumor has been quashed. Maybe we should buy some more, too."

Sebastian laughed bitterly. "With what? I have nothing left, and I still owe fifteen thousand guilders. Do you have any idea where I can borrow such a sum?"

Zuzarte shook his head sadly. "I wish I did, but I don't. If only I had the money, I would lend it to you myself. But we'll get through this. You'll see. The coffee market is strong now. And the burden of protecting it and supporting the price no longer falls on you alone. From now on, all your friends and associates who invested in coffee out of respect and friendship for you will have a stake in supporting the price. You're not alone any more. You have many allies, and some of them are very rich. Come now, isn't this wonderful news?"

"Yes, I suppose it is. But I find it difficult to take pleasure in it right now."

"Can't you ask any of your friends?" said Zuzarte.

"I wouldn't have the audacity," said Sebastian. "They've put a lot of money into coffee as a favor to me. How can I ask them for loans on top of all that?"

"Even if you borrow one thousand from fifteen different people?"

"I just can't. A thousand guilders is also a lot of money. I need new sources, and I can't think of any. And I need the money fast. If I don't deliver the money to Johannes Hoogaboom by tomorrow, he'll drive me into bankruptcy."

"Don't despair," said Zuzarte. "Something will come up. We're almost there. Everything is falling into place. Look, we've weathered every crisis so far. One way or another, the money will come, and then you'll be able to relax. You'll see. We'll celebrate tomorrow."

Sebastian was not reassured by Zuzarte's words of encouragement. He did not go home until the closing bell rang, even though he did not realistically expect any new developments. His face felt flushed as he walked, and his heart pounded against his chest. His throat was constricted with a fear unlike any he had ever known. He had faced death with bravery and courage on more than one occasion, but what he faced now was humiliation and a life shattered into little pieces, a living death. It called for a courage that he didn't possess.

In desperation, his thoughts turned in a direction he had refused even to consider. There was one person who had fifteen thousand guilders and would lend it to him if he asked. It was his mother.

Doña Angelica had received thirty thousand guilders of the money Don Pedro had left his family, and she still had it. The money was invested conservatively, and it brought her a modest profit. And she had no expenses. Sebastian paid for the house and he took care of the household expenses. Felipe had an additional fifteen thousand guilders. If he asked either of them, they would lend him the money without a second thought.

He could not ask Felipe, on the threshold of his wedding, to lend him all the money he had in the world. And he certainly couldn't ask him for anything while he lay wounded in bed fighting for his life. But he could ask his mother. Fifteen thousand guilders was only part of her fortune. She would lend it to him gladly.

Doña Angelica had tea and cakes ready for him when he came in. They drank their tea and chatted about inconsequential things for a while, but Doña Angelica could sense his agitation.

"Sebastian, what's on your mind?" she said.

He was about to ask her, but at the very last moment, he just couldn't bring himself to do it.

"It's nothing, Mother."

"It's not nothing. I'm your mother, and I know when something is nothing. This is not nothing."

"It's just a business matter," said Sebastian, his eyes downcast, unable to meet hers. "It's really not that important."

"Sebastian! Talk to me. I've never seen you so disturbed. You were about to say something to me, and then you changed your mind. I saw it on your face. I want to know what you were going to say to me. I insist."

Sebastian looked up. "You are my mother, and I have to obey you. But I really would prefer that we don't talk about it."

"Sebastian, you are right. I am your mother, and I love you very much. I want to know what happened and what you wanted to tell me. I have a right to know."

"Very well," he said. "This is the situation I'm in. I invested in coffee heavily, and there were problems in the market that drew me in much deeper than I had intended. I don't want to go into all the details, but everything I have is sitting in coffee, and in addition, I owe a lot of money."

Doña Angelica took a deep breath and let it out slowly. "How is the coffee market now?"

"It's stable. It even went up a little bit today."

"So it will work out for you, Sebastian. You'll pay off your debts from the profits you make."

Sebastian shook his head. "It's not so simple. Johannes Hoogaboom at the Bank of Amsterdam has called in my line of credit. If I don't pay off by tomorrow, he'll push me into bankruptcy."

Doña Angelica was quiet for a moment or two. "I see," she finally said, her voice barely above a whisper. "How much do you owe the bank?"

"Fifteen thousand guilders."

"And you were going to ask me to lend you the money, and then you decided against it."

"Yes."

"But I want to lend you the money, Sebastian. The money means nothing to me. Your happiness and peace of mind are more important to me than all the money in the world."

"I can't take it, Mother."

"But I insist. I want you to take it. But I don't want to lend to you. I give it to you as a gift."

"I can't take the money from you, Mother. Not as a loan and not as a gift."

"Look at it as my wedding gift to you, Sebastian. Maybe it's a little early, but it's my wedding gift to you."

"It's wonderful of you to offer, but I can't take it."

"Why not?"

"I would not be able to live with the shame and the dishonor if I took your money under these circumstances."

"But no one would know."

"I would know, Mother. I would know."

Doña Angelica bit her lower lip, and her eyes misted with tears.

"I do understand," she said. "You are your father's son. Proud and courageous. And always honorable. Is there no one else from whom you could borrow this money?"

Sebastian shook his head.

"Wait, I have an idea," she said. "Why don't you ask Senhor Setubal? He has a lot of money, more money than he can count. I'm sure that lending you fifteen thousand guilders will not be a great hardship for him."

"I can't, Mother. I hardly know him."

"Why not? You've met a few times. He likes you, and you like him. He might even become your stepfather one day. You could just talk to him about it man to man. It's not as if you have no prospects for repaying the loan. When the ship comes in, you'll have more than enough to pay him back."

"I just can't, Mother."

"Do you want me to ask him for you?"

"Mother," he said. "Mother."

She sank down, deflated. "I know, Sebastian. I'm sorry. It was just a thought, a desperate thought. How can I help you? Tell me what to do."

"There's nothing you can do for me now."

"So what are you going to do?"

"There's one more place I can try, Mother."

An hour later, Sebastian knocked on the door of the Castillo home. The maid let him in and asked him to wait in the parlor while she announced his arrival.

Senhora Castillo came bustling in.

"Sebastian, what a pleasant surprise. We weren't expecting you. I'm sorry, but Dulce is not home. If we knew you were coming …"

"Actually, I came to speak with Senhor Castillo. Is he home?"

"Is everything all right?" she asked with sudden concern.

"It's just a business matter," he said.

"Oh," she said, relieved. "I'll get my husband. Give my best to your mother. Such an extraordinary woman."

Sebastian paced back and forth as he waited for his future father-in-law. He felt a surge of panic in his throat and an urge to flee, but before he could do anything about it, Miguel Castillo entered the room.

"Sebastian, how nice to see you," he said with genuine warmth. "My wife tells me that you wanted to discuss some business with me."

"Yes, I do."

For the next half hour, Sebastian gave his future father-in-law a full report on everything that had happened to his investment in the coffee market. He did not dwell on the persecutions his family was suffering at the hands of Salazar, but regarding the investment, he did not leave out a single detail.

"So you see," he concluded, "everything I have is invested in coffee. But the market has stabilized, and the prospects are good. And there are a number of people who are now as interested as I am in the stability of the coffee market. But right now I am in a tight corner."

"And you want me to lend you the money?" said Castillo.

"I am mortified and humiliated to ask you for this loan, but I really have no time and nowhere to turn. If I don't come to the bank with the money tomorrow, I will be ruined. All the people I might have asked have already bought into coffee to help me support the price. I can't ask them for loans. My mother offered to lend me the money, but I cannot sink so low."

"I understand," said Castillo. "I am definitely a more honorable choice for you. And I appreciate how difficult this is for you, Sebastian." He scratched his right ear. "I have to think."

Sebastian rose to go. "When shall I —?"

"Sit down, young man," said Castillo. "I didn't mean for you to go. I'll do my thinking right here and now."

Castillo leaned back, closed his eyes and pursed his lips. He remained perfectly still for a long time, the sound of his breathing measured and even. Sebastian folded his hands in his lap, looked down at his feet and waited in silence.

"Sebastian," said Castillo.

Sebastian's head snapped up, and he looked at Castillo.

"Sebastian, you are already like a son to me," said Castillo, "and I want to help you. You understand that you are in a precarious position. The coffee market may seem stable now, but it could change overnight. Your actions have been out of character for you, but these things can happen. Young men are sometimes caught up in the excitement of new frontiers in business, or anything else for that matter, and prudence can fall by the wayside. I understand, and I really hope that things work out well for you."

"Thank you."

"As far as a loan is concerned, we need to do this on a business basis, so that it does not become an embarrassment for either of us."

"Absolutely," said Sebastian. "I agree."

"So what security can you give me for my money?"

"I've thought about this, and I'm willing to transfer half of my holdings to you in return for fifteen thousand guilders. I have several times that invested in the coffee shares, but I will gladly give up half my shares in order to clear myself with the bank."

Castillo stroked his chin. "That is a good offer. But it is too risky for me. How do I have an assurance that I will get my money back?"

Sebastian had nothing more to offer.

"The only assurance I can give you," he said, "is my word of honor. No matter what happens, I will repay the loan."

Castillo nodded. "That is an acceptable assurance. I will give you the loan."

One week later, reports reached Amsterdam of French military maneuvers near Charleroi in the Spanish Netherlands. Within hours, these reports gave rise to rumors of an impending

French invasion of the Netherlands. War fever spread through the Dutch capital like wildfire. The government issued proclamations that there was no impending war, but the people were skeptical of the denials. Concerned about the disruptions of war, they emptied the markets of flour and other staples.

On the Exchange, war fever brought upheaval and dislocation to the markets. The price of wheat skyrocketed. Traders abandoned all commodities that would not be essential to the war effort. Munitions and the textiles needed for uniforms drew enormous trading activity. Sugar and whiskey held their own, with just moderate declines. But the market for coffee collapsed entirely. No one needed coffee or had any interest in it when the storm clouds of war were gathering on the horizon.

Within a day, Sebastian was completely wiped out. The coffee shares he held were barely worth the paper on which they were written, and he was left with a debt of fifteen thousand guilders to his future father-in-law with no prospect in sight of how he could ever repay it. All his friends and associates who had bought coffee to help him support the market suffered heavy financial losses. Although they were far from ruined, they gave him cold stares and turned away when he passed by at the Exchange. The Jewish traders who supported him were especially upset, because the coffee fiasco had embarrassed them and caused them to lose credibility with the gentile traders on the Exchange.

Defeated and humiliated, Sebastian did not venture out of his house all that day. He just sat in a chair and stared at the walls with unseeing eyes, his mind and heart numbed beyond thought and feeling. Doña Angelica longed to comfort him, but she knew that the time for consolation had not yet arrived.

The next day, Sebastian was still in his numbed state when Eduardo Colon knocked on the door. Sebastian had no choice but to pull himself together and fulfill his social obligation to receive the *parnas* cordially.

Colon was waiting in the parlor when Doña Angelica and Sebastian came in.

"My apologies for intruding at such a time," said Colon. "I know that it is not the most joyful of times in the Dominguez household. But I have certain duties to perform that cannot wait for another day."

Doña Angelica arched her eyebrows, but did not say a word.

"First of all, Senhor Dominguez," continued Colon, "I must express my distress at the unfortunate events at the Exchange that resulted from your dabbling in coffee. If you have not yet heard, the rumors of war have proved false, as rumors often do. Sanity has returned to the Exchange this morning. But the price of coffee will not recover for a very long time. All the recent fluctuations have made the market leery of coffee. And after the collapse of the coffee market yesterday, even though it was caused by a false rumor, no one is interested in coffee anymore. Tea will do just fine."

"I appreciate your telling this to me," said Sebastian in a dull monotone.

"Why have you come here, senhor?" said Doña Angelica. "Is it to rub salt in our wounds?"

"Certainly not, senhora," said Colon. "Your son should understand what damage he has caused. First, he invested recklessly in coffee shares, and then he scrambled to secure his investment by pouring more money into it to support the prices. He even instructed agents in other cities to buy up coffee shares — on credit! — so that he could artificially prop up the market. Then he borrowed a huge sum of money to cover his debts, a loan which he cannot repay now that the market has collapsed. And he also convinced many people to come to his aid and invest their money in coffee —

even though he knew it was an unstable market. And now these people, many of them Christian traders, have lost their investment. Our community has been humiliated. We have been watching his market manipulations with disapproval, trepidation and concern for quite a while now, but this is the last straw."

"But why have you come here today?" said Sebastian. "What is the purpose of your visit?"

"I am getting to the point," said Colon. "I'll be there in a minute. But first I must perform a rather unpleasant duty."

He turned to Doña Angelica.

"Senhora Dominguez, I am the bearer of a message," he said, "that is just for you. Do you want me to convey the message in front of your son?"

"Speak freely, senhor," she said.

"The message is from Senhor Setubal," said Colon. "He asked me to express his high esteem for you, but he regrets that in light of the scandal in which your son is involved he will no longer be able to consider a relationship with the Dominguez family. He begs your forgiveness and asks for your understanding. He asked me to convey to you his sympathy and high regard."

Tears welled up in Doña Angelica's eyes, and she bit her lower lip to keep from crying. She squared her shoulders and took a deep breath.

"I'm so sorry, Mother," said Sebastian, his voice cracking. "I'm so sorry."

"And I am sorry, senhora," said Colon, "to carry this message. Senhor Setubal was very upset. This is not something that he wanted to do. But ... please forgive me. I was the one who initiated this match, and it is my unfortunate task to bring it to an end."

"I understand, senhor," said Doña Angelica, her voice shaky but controlled. "Now that you've delivered the message, can you please get to the point of this visit? We will need our privacy."

"Of course," said Colon. "If you recall, when you first came to Amsterdam, we explained to you that the Maamad has the sacred duty of protecting the integrity of the community. I have come to tell you that Senhor Sebastian Dominguez is hereby summoned to the Maamad for a hearing."

"A hearing?" said Sebastian, his heart in his throat. "About what?"

"It has been proposed that we put you in *cherem* for the damage you have caused to the community."

# THE HEARING ROOM · 15

THE HEARING ROOM OF THE MAAMAD was so crowded that a number of people had to step out into the hall to allow Rabbi Aboab and Rabbi Sasportas to enter and take their seats. Every inch of space was occupied by people connected to the hearing as well as spectators. Even though it was a brisk autumn day, the windows were opened slightly from the bottom to let in some air, and groups of people who could not get into the room clustered around them.

Eduardo Colon took his seat at the council table, Yakob Santos to his right and Martino Vega to his left. In honor of the occasion, Colon wore a satin suit of royal blue with gold trim; scarlet or yellow would have been inappropriate considering the gravity of the proceedings. He banged on the table for quiet.

"Silence! Silence!" he shouted. "Anyone talking during these proceedings will be asked to leave the room."

The noise of conversation ebbed and finally disappeared.

"Revered rabbis," Colon began with a bow toward the venerable sages, "we are honored that you have joined us today to observe the proceedings. We are like dust beneath your feet, and any time you wish to make a comment or remark, feel free to do so. We thirst for your words of wisdom."

The two old rabbis nodded to him, and he continued.

"Fellow members of the Naçao, our cherished community, the hearing we are about to hold is in regard to Senhor

Sebastian Dominguez, one of our newer members. At his request, we called for the attendance of everyone who is even remotely connected with the events that are about to be described, and we wish to express our appreciation to all of you who have taken the trouble to come here today. I find it truly amazing."

Colon was indeed amazed as he looked around and saw all the people who had come. Doña Angelica and Sebastian were there, of course. Felipe was still too weak to attend. Felipe's fiancée Rebecca was there, with her parents, Emanuel and Sarah Pinto, as was Sebastian's fiancée Dulce and her parents, Miguel and Maite Castillo. Next to them sat Sergio Setubal, and then Rabbi Mordechai Strasbourg, Amos Strasbourg and Netzach Tomashov. Behind them sat Diego Zuzarte, Johannes and Wilhelmina Hoogaboom, Gonzalo Sanchez, Roelof Groesbeck and Piet Vanderweghe.

"Thank you all for coming," Colon said again. "I know it must have been difficult for some of you." He cleared his throat and shuffled the papers in front of him. "Well, let's get on with it. The question under consideration is the proper response of the Maamad to Senhor Dominguez's actions over the past months. He is charged with reckless manipulation of the market to the detriment of many members of our community and quite a few Christians as well."

For the next five minutes, he enumerated the charges in minute detail.

"The scandal has been damaging to the community," he continued. "Not only have many individuals suffered losses unjustly, the community as a whole has been humiliated and discredited in the eyes of our Christian friends and neighbors. Therefore, it has been proposed that Senhor Dominguez be put in *cherem*. It is our duty here to decide if we should indeed excommunicate him, and if so, whether the excommunication should be permanent or for a specific period of time."

There was a sudden gasp in the room. It came from Dulce Castillo. Sebastian looked at her, but she turned for comfort to her mother instead.

"We have with us today," continued Colon, "a respected Ashkenazi rabbi, Rabbi Mordechai Strasbourg, one of the most distinguished rabbis of our sister community here in Amsterdam. Rabbi Strasbourg has asked for permission to make a presentation in defense of Senhor Dominguez, and permission has, of course, been granted. Rabbi Strasbourg, *kavod*, the floor is yours."

Rabbi Strasbourg rose to his feet and went to stand along-side the council table. His manner was sober and grave.

"Revered rabbis, honored *parnassim*, members of the community, citizens of Amsterdam," he began, "the events that Senhor Colon described to you are part of a larger story, and you cannot understand them unless you know it. I want to tell you that story.

"We all know the story of the Dominguez family. We know about Don Pedro, who gave his life to sanctify the Name of the Almighty. We know that his family was in Paris when he and Sebastian were arrested by the Inquisition and that his family remained there under the protection of King Louis XIV. We know about Sebastian's spectacular escape from prison in Spain and his reunion with his family in Paris. But from that time on, most of you know very little about the experiences of the Dominguez family.

"When Sebastian was attending his sister's wedding in Hamburg, he made a last-minute decision to visit my cousin, Rabbi Shlomo Strasbourg, in Vienna. He traveled incognito, as a German Jew from Hamburg, but as soon as he got to Vienna he was arrested and thrown into prison. He would have been sent back to Spain if King Jan Sobieski had not rescued Vienna from the Turks and set Sebastian free as a favor to my cousin. Someone betrayed Sebastian.

"Who betrayed Sebastian and tried to get him sent back to Spain? And why?

"As soon as Sebastian was released from prison in Vienna, he heard that his mother, the gracious Doña Angelica, had been accused of witchcraft in Metz. Rushing back to be at her side, he was attacked on the road by highwaymen. They tried to steal his saddlebags which contained a safe passage from the King of Poland. There was a battle and one of the highwaymen was killed, but as he was dying he revealed that he was hired by a man named Karl.

"Who was this Karl? Who sent him?

"Sebastian came back to Metz and discovered that the accusation arose because Doña Angelica's housekeeper observed her doing something to protect against an *ayin hara*, an evil eye. The housekeeper reported it to her priest. It was really a trivial matter, a bit of silliness that should have been cleared up quickly and easily; it should never have led to an accusation of witchcraft. But it did, and if she had been tried and convicted, she would have been executed. And as much as the family tried to bring the matter to an end, there were unseen forces behind the scenes pressing for a witch trial. Doña Angelica only avoided a trial when Sebastian showed the King of France the safe passage he received from the King of Poland for himself and his entire family. This was the very same safe passage that the highwaymen tried to steal from him on the road to Metz.

"Who tried to deprive the Dominguez family of their safe passage? Who exerted tremendous pressure behind the scenes to bring Doña Angelica to trial for witchcraft and perhaps to have her executed?

"The family finally arrived in Amsterdam. Don Pedro had left them a large sum of money with a friend. It was in the form of letters of credit. On the day Sebastian went to the bank to deposit the money, he was attacked by Karl and a man named Steen. They knocked him down and stole his pouch, but fortunately, the letters of credit were in his pocket and not in his pouch.

"Who sent Karl to steal the Dominguez money?

"Sebastian deposited the money. He joined the Exchange and invested his money prudently and conservatively. It was against his nature to gamble and take high risks. He earned a reputation as a capable young trader with sound judgment and a bright future, and he gained the respect of the community. And then there was a false rumor of a hurricane in Jamaica that promised to drive up the price of sugar. He was tempted to invest a little money in sugar and make a quick profit, as was just about everyone on the Exchange, but a young trader named Diego Zuzarte — he is sitting right there — convinced him that the rumor was false and that he would lose money if he invested. Zuzarte turned out to be right, and Sebastian was appreciative.

"Soon afterward, Sebastian was walking to the Exchange with Zuzarte when a wagon almost ran him down. Zuzarte pushed him aside at the last second and saved his life. Now he really saw Zuzarte as his friend. The man had saved his life! But it was all a lie, a ploy to gain Sebastian's trust and confidence. Karl hired Zuzarte to worm his way into Sebastian's trust, and he planted the false rumor about the hurricane in Jamaica, so that Zuzarte could save Sebastian from a bad investment. And Karl ran the wagon at Sebastian so that Zuzarte could make believe he had saved Sebastian's life and gain even more of his trust."

"How do you know this, rabbi?" said Colon. "Senhor Zuzarte sits right there, and you are accusing him. Shouldn't he have the right to defend himself?"

"Absolutely," said Rabbi Strasbourg. "Senhor Zuzarte, would you like to tell this august gathering what you told me last night?"

All eyes turned to Zuzarte, and he sank down in his chair, as if he could blend into the wooden slats and disappear completely. But he knew there was no escape. He would have to swallow the bitter pill of public humiliation if he wanted to avoid more dire consequences.

With a deep sigh, he pulled himself to his feet. The room was immediately abuzz with whispers and murmurs, but a stern look and a sharp rap on the table by Colon quickly restored order.

"It is true," said Zuzarte. "All the rabbi said is true. The rabbi figured out what happened and said he would tell everything at the hearing today. He said that if I cooperated it would go better for me. I swear I knew nothing about the evil scheme in which I became involved. I thought it was just a little market manipulation, you know, taking advantage of unsuspecting investors. It happens all the time. I know it was wrong, and I'm prepared to make amends, but I swear I knew nothing about the terrible scheme into which I'd been drawn."

"Would you like to tell us what happened?"

Zuzarte shrugged and shifted his feet. He avoided Sebastian's angry eyes.

"This man Karl approached me," he said. "He wanted me to do something and promised to pay me well. He gave me a lot of money just to listen to him and said there would be much more when the job was done. It's just as the rabbi said. He planted the rumor about the hurricane so that I could stop Senhor Dominguez from investing, and he ran the wagon at him so that it would seem I saved his life. Once I had Senhor Dominguez's trust, my job was to draw him into a large investment in coffee. Then Karl dumped a large block of coffee shares on the market through a broker named Coronal. I convinced Senhor Dominguez to buy them up to protect his investment."

"Was Karl doing this on his own?" asked the rabbi.

"No, there was someone behind him."

"Who was it?"

"I don't know," said Zuzarte. "He never said."

The rabbi nodded. "Continue please."

"As time went on," said Zuzarte, "Karl manufactured more eruptions in coffee, and each time I convinced Senhor Dominguez, sometimes directly, sometimes by subterfuge, that he should put in more money to protect his investment. And the deeper he was drawn into the quicksand of coffee, the more desperate he became and the more likely to sink even deeper. I convinced him to give standing instructions to agents in different cities to support the price of coffee by making purchases for him on credit. So now he had not only sunk all his money into coffee, he was also deeply in debt.

"Karl then planted a rumor that there was a second ship coming in from the East Indies with a boatload of coffee. The price of coffee was threatened again, and I convinced Senhor Dominguez that to prevent a collapse he had to ask his friends and associates to buy into coffee and help him support the price. And that was what he did. He is a respected man, and people helped him, especially because he assured them that in the end they'd profit handsomely. So now he was even deeper in the hole. All his money was invested in coffee. He was heavily in debt to the bank. And he had drawn his friends and associates in with him.

"Then Johannes Hoogaboom at the bank called in Senhor Dominguez's credit line. He had no way to pay it off. All the people to whom he might have gone for a loan had already done him the favor of buying into coffee to prop up the price. He couldn't go back to them for loans. And Karl assured me that he wouldn't ask his mother. His employer — whose identity I still do not know — had explained to him that Senhor Dominguez's sense of honor would not allow him to do it. Senhor Dominguez would have no choice but to ask Senhor Castillo, his future father-in-law, which is what Karl's employer wanted."

"Didn't you get the feeling, Senhor Zuzarte," said the rabbi, "that there was something more sinister going on here than one of your innocent market manipulations to take advantage of unsuspecting investors, as you call them?"

"I did, rabbi," said Zuzarte. "I was getting very uncomfortable with the way things were developing. Karl was driving Senhor Dominguez into ruin, and that was never my intention. I am not a malicious man. A little greedy perhaps, but not malicious."

"So why didn't you put a stop to it?"

"I couldn't," said Zuzarte. "I was in too deep. And Karl threatened to kill me if I said a word to anyone."

"But now you don't need to worry about Karl because he is dead?"

"Yes. He is dead."

"All right, go on with your gruesome story," said the rabbi.

Zuzarte took a deep breath. "There's not much else to tell. After Senhor Dominguez borrowed the money from Senhor Castillo and cleared his account with the bank, Karl planted the war rumors. That drove the market into a frenzy, and coffee, which was an unstable market under the best of circumstances because its use is not yet widespread in Europe, completely collapsed. And it is unlikely to recover for a long time. Senhor Dominguez was effectively ruined, and he had also caused heavy financial losses to quite a few other people. Karl's work was complete, and I had been forced to play a part in it. I am so sorry. I beg forgiveness from everyone I hurt and from the Almighty in Heaven above."

"And you have no idea who was behind Karl?"

"No idea whatsoever," said Zuzarte. "I swear it."

"All right, Senhor Zuzarte, you may sit down," said the rabbi. He looked around the packed hearing room. Everyone looked at him with rapt attention. There was not a sound to be heard. "So the story unfolds before our horrified eyes. Someone has woven a web and drawn Sebastian into it.

"Who was behind Karl?

"Who drove Sebastian into ruin?

"Who is this evil spider?

"But we are not finished. Because there is something even more sinister going on here. The Dominguez family is not only being driven into financial ruin but also into social ruin. A scandal such as this can lead to the pronouncement of *cherem*, which is being considered right here. Before all this happened, it seemed that Doña Angelica was on the verge of an engagement to Senhor Sergio Setubal, but yesterday, he felt forced to send his regrets. And how long would it be before the Castillo family broke the engagement with Sebastian? And could the Pinto family hold back from breaking the engagement with Felipe? Scandal is a pernicious thing.

"Yes, this evil spider was out to destroy the Dominguez family financially, socially and perhaps even physically. I'm sure everyone has heard about the knife attack on Felipe Dominguez. He is recovering, thank Heaven, and our prayers are with him, but he could easily have been killed.

"Who was behind the attack? And why did he want Felipe killed?

"And then there is the final episode in this sordid saga. A few nights ago, this evil spider called Karl to a rendez-vous in a small Catholic church in the extreme northeast of Amsterdam, and he stabbed him to death. Why did he kill Karl? It was obvious. The job was done. Karl had accomplished what he had been hired to do, and now he no longer served a useful purpose. He was just a liability, and the spider squashed him like a bug.

"It also turns out that the housekeeper of the Dominguez family for years, a woman named Helga who is actually Karl's sister, was planted in their household to spy on them. She told Karl about Sebastian's plans to travel incognito to Vienna, and Karl was able to betray him. On Karl's instructions, she also told the priest about Doña Angelica's attempt to ward off the evil eye and construed it as witchcraft. Then when they came to Amsterdam, she told Karl when Sebastian would be taking his money to the bank so that Karl could waylay and rob him. She has admitted to all of this, and she is now under arrest."

The rabbi took a sip of water. The crowd held its collective breath.

"So who is this evil spider? Who is this mysterious presence that lurks in the background and sends out hirelings to do his evil work?

"What do we know about him? According to the priest of the church in the northeast of Amsterdam, he calls himself Salazar, he has been coming to that church for a long time, he prays there and he makes generous contributions. All indications are that Salazar is a Catholic. We also know that he is tall. Senhor Gonzalo Sanchez followed Karl to the rendezvous at the church. He saw Salazar from afar, but Salazar slipped away through the back door of the church.

"What else do we know about Salazar, our evil spider?

"We know what he attempted to do. He betrayed Sebastian and tried to get him sent back to Spain where he would undoubtedly have been put to death. So it seems he wanted Sebastian dead. But wait! When Karl and his men attacked Sebastian on the road to Metz they only tried to steal his saddlebags. They could have killed him, but they didn't. And then again, when they waylaid Sebastian in Amsterdam and stole his pouch, they could have killed him, but they didn't. So did Salazar want Sebastian dead or didn't he?

"Salazar plotted to have Doña Angelica put on trial for witchcraft, and we can assume he would have done his utmost to have her convicted if she had gone to trial. So he was trying to kill her. But he could have had her killed many times, and he didn't. So did he want her dead or didn't he?

"And then Salazar orders one of his men to attack Felipe — and kill him! There could be no doubt about that. The killer threw a knife at Felipe's back and just missed his heart. So Salazar is ambivalent about killing Doña Angelica and Sebastian. Sometimes it seems he wants them dead, and sometimes it seems he doesn't. But he tries to kill Felipe, no question about it. And if he wants to kill Felipe, why wait for years to do it? He could have done it back in Paris or Metz. Why wait until just recently to kill Felipe?

"What is going on in Salazar's mind? What are his motives?

"And then it struck me." He paused, and everyone leaned forward to catch his words. "Salazar was out for revenge. What motivated him? Hatred. Pure, vitriolic hatred. He wanted revenge, and he wanted to savor every moment of it. He wanted the Dominguez family to suffer. A quick death would not satisfy him. He wanted Sebastian to be arrested and sent back to an Inquisition prison. He wanted him to be tortured and to live with horror and anguish until he was finally burned at the stake. Killing him on the highway or in an Amsterdam alleyway was too easy and too quick.

"And he wanted Doña Angelica to suffer. He wanted her to be arrested and put on trial for witchcraft. He wanted her to experience fear and despair and finally to be burned as a witch. Of course, he could have killed her many times, but that would not have satisfied his ravenous appetite for revenge.

"And when the Dominguez family finally arrived in Amsterdam, he plotted and schemed to take his revenge on them by embroiling them in scandal and driving them into financial and social ruin.

"And why did he try to kill Felipe by a quick stab in the back? Because he had no interest in Felipe. He wanted revenge on Doña Angelica and Sebastian. And he knew that if he killed Felipe they would suffer unbearable grief and sorrow. This was supposed to be the *coup de grâce*, the final touch to his sweet revenge. The family, in ruins financially and socially, broken and demoralized, suffers the murder of the younger son. The pain would be beyond belief, and that was exactly what Salazar wanted.

"What an evil, diabolical spider! What a monster!

"But who is Salazar? What is his real name?

"So let us examine his motives a little more closely. He doesn't care about Felipe. The targets of his revenge are Doña Angelica and Sebastian. What have these two done to this man that he should hate them so much? Why do they deserve this terrible assault?

"This question baffled me, and once I saw the answer, everything fell into place. Salazar was not looking for revenge against Doña Angelica and Sebastian. He wanted revenge against Don Pedro. But Don Pedro was dead and beyond his reach, so instead, he decided to wreak his vengeance on Don Pedro's wife and his firstborn son. In his mind, they represented Don Pedro. They were Don Pedro incarnate. They had to be, because otherwise, how would he have his revenge?"

The door opened. Three Dutch constables came into the hearing room and took up positions in front of the door. The rabbi nodded to them.

"So we are getting closer to Salazar," said the rabbi. "We know that he is tall, that he is a Catholic and that he bears a terrible grudge against Don Pedro. But we also know something else about him. The Maamad does not allow contact between the members of the Naçao and the gentile population other than strictly business matters. But Salazar seems to have a lot of knowledge about what is going on in the community and the social relationships.

"Who was his contact in the community? It couldn't be Karl, because he was a German gentile. So who could it be? And why would a Catholic living in Amsterdam for a long time bear such a horrendous grudge against Don Pedro who was here for only a short time many years ago?

"No, the grudge has to go back to Spain. Don Pedro did something in Spain that ignited Salazar's hatred. So this Salazar must have lived or spent a lot of time in Spain a long time ago. Then something happened, and he became filled with hatred for Don Pedro and sought to take his revenge against Don Pedro's widow and firstborn son. But how many Catholics living in Amsterdam are originally from Spain? Hardly any, I would say.

"There could be only one answer to these questions. Salazar is a member of the Naçao community here in Amsterdam. He is descended from a *converso* family, but he is not a secret Jew. He is a faithful Catholic masquerading as a former Marrano. And his identity is also obvious.

"There he is!" shouted the rabbi as he pointed his finger. "Sergio Setubal! He is the guilty one. He is the evil spider. He is Salazar!"

Sergio Setubal stole a glance at the Dutch constables and smiled at the rabbi indulgently. "You paint a pretty picture, rabbi," he said. "But there is not an ounce of truth in it. And not a shred of evidence."

"We will see, Senhor Setubal," said the rabbi. "We will see."

"Why don't you continue?" said Setubal. "This is entertaining, watching a rabbi make such a fool of himself in public."

"Enjoy your entertainment while you can, Senhor Setubal," said the rabbi. He turned to the *parnassim* at the council table. "Please excuse this interruption. I will continue. So what do we know about Sergio Setubal? We know that he came here about ten years ago from Spain where he lived as a secret Jew in Ocaña, a small town some distance from Madrid and Toledo with hardly any Marrano population, if any at all. We know that his wife died under the torturer's knife in an Inquisition prison. We know that his wife was sickly and could never bear him any children. We know that he escaped from Spain one step ahead of the Inquisition. We know that he came to Amsterdam where the Setubal family, his relatives, helped him get started in business. And we also know that he has become very wealthy here in Amsterdam.

"But how do we know all this? What is our source of information? There is only one source. Sergio Setubal! We have his word and absolutely nothing else. No one remembers him from Ocaña. No one saw him worshiping as a secret Jew in Spain. No one knows anything about him except that his name is Setubal and that he is descended from a family of *conversos*. But most of the *conversos* became faithful Catholics. No one knows that his wife was arrested by the Inquisition. No one knows any of this. Because it is all a lie.

"Sergio Setubal is a faithful Catholic descended from *conversos*. We know nothing about his family. If he had a wife, and if his wife died, she may have done so from any of a thousand causes. For some reason, he had to leave Spain, so he came to Amsterdam where he knew he had distant cousins in the former Marrano community. He told them his story and gained their sympathy. They welcomed him into the community, and he became a reverse Marrano, a secret Catholic living in a Jewish community. But he didn't give up his faith completely. He found an obscure Catholic church in a remote corner of the city, and he went there to practice his religion.

"It was not hard for him to masquerade as a former Marrano. Almost all Marranos escaping from Spain and

Portugal do not know how to read Hebrew or any of the prayers or the holy texts. They just know the Old Testament as it appears in the Christian Bible and some of the customs, such as lighting candles and abstaining from pork. Here in Amsterdam, Setubal studied to become a Jew so that he could keep up his masquerade, but he never married, because he had no interest in raising a Jewish family.

"The only match he entertained was to Doña Angelica. He manipulated people to persuade Rabbi Aboab that it was time for her to remarry and that Setubal would be a good choice. He also persuaded Senhor Colon to suggest the match. His plan was to become engaged to her and, when the scandal broke, to break off the engagement and break her heart. It would be another delicious twist of the knife of revenge. When the scandal broke and they were still not engaged, he sent her a message that he was no longer interested. It was the next best thing to breaking off the engagement."

Doña Angelica burst into tears, and the rabbi stopped to give her a chance to regain her composure. The hearing room remained perfectly silent. After a brief moment of weakness, Doña Angelica squared her shoulders and wiped her eyes. She smiled wanly at the rabbi and nodded.

"I am so sorry, Senhora Dominguez," said the rabbi, "that I must cause you such pain, and in public, but we must cauterize this wound once and for all." He looked around the room. "Here before you is the monster who calls himself Salazar. His real name is Sergio Setubal."

"You have no proof," said Setubal. "Send letters to the Marrano community in Toledo, and you will discover that everything you said is a lie. I am no more a Catholic than you are."

"We will see about that," said the rabbi. He nodded to the constables. One of them opened the door, and a priest came into the hearing room.

"Welcome and thank you for coming," said the rabbi. "Would you please introduce yourself?"

"I am Father Lodewijk Schermerhorn of the Church of Saint Jerome," said the priest. "It is a small Catholic church in the northeast."

"Has a man called Salazar been coming to your church?"

"Yes. For years and years."

"Has he ever come with a man called Karl?"

"Yes. Karl Schmidt," said the priest. "Karl was murdered in my church just the other day. Stabbed in the back. A dreadful business."

"Do you see Senhor Salazar anywhere in this room?"

The priest scanned the faces carefully as his eyes moved across the crowded room.

"There he is," he said. "That is Senhor Salazar."

His finger pointed directly at Sergio Setubal.

Setubal leaped to his feet. He saw that the door was blocked by the Dutch constables. He turned to the windows, but the crowd blocked his access to those as well. His face became a mask of fury and hatred. All traces of the kindly and elegant gentleman were gone.

"So you've found me out," he snarled. "It doesn't matter. You're too late. I've had my revenge. And you're right, rabbi, it was oh so sweet. I watched the wicked man's wife and son twist and turn in agony every time I applied the pressure, and it was such a pleasure. But now my pleasure will be complete, because I'll reveal the reason they've suffered so much. They'll remember their suffering forever, and they'll know at whose door to lay the blame."

"Why don't you tell us what this is all about?" said the rabbi.

"Oh, I will, I will," said Setubal. "There's no longer any point in secrecy. On the contrary, I want you to know. That's the finishing touch to my revenge. Because what good is revenge if your victim doesn't know what it was all about?

"I had a family in Ocaña. My wife died of an illness, but I have grown children. I always had a little money, but I was never rich. And then I had an opportunity to become really wealthy and have everything I ever wanted. A grand house, carriages and fine horses, servants, respect and status in the community, everything.

"How was I going to do this? By selling uniforms and boots to the Spanish army. It cost me everything I had and more. I had to borrow very heavily from everyone I knew, because I needed a lot of money to make the venture work. I had to buy the materials and the manufacturing equipment, and more important, I had to distribute lavish gifts to many officials in order to get the contracts. You would call them bribes, but I prefer to call them gifts. The cost was very high, but it didn't matter. The prices I negotiated with these officials were going to give me enormous profits even after all these costs.

"And then, just as I was about to go into production, Don Pedro put a stop to everything. He canceled the contracts, because he could get the uniforms and boots produced for a fraction of the cost in Asturias. The government would save a lot of money, but I would be left out in the cold. I begged him. I pleaded with him. I offered him half my profits. I even offered him all my profits if he would at least let me recover the money I had invested. But he refused to listen. He said it was his duty to the Crown to bring down the expenses of the military.

"That pompous, arrogant man ruined me. There was no way I could ever recover all the gifts I had distributed to the officials, and there was no way I could ever repay the money I had borrowed from anyone and everyone. I was ruined and humiliated. I couldn't face my family, my neighbors, my community. I was like a walking dead man. All I could do was leave Spain and try to make my fortune in Amsterdam, which I did with the help of my Jewish cousins. But I vowed to have my revenge. He ruined my life, and I vowed to ruin his.

"I planned and schemed, but it never occurred to me that Don Pedro of all people was really a secret Jew and that he would be burned at the stake. The Inquisition robbed me of my vengeance. But I was not to be denied. If I couldn't destroy Don Pedro, I could destroy his widow and his first-born. And I did.

"Now you can do with me as you wish." He nodded to the constables. "Just take me by my house. I need a few things."

The constables took Setubal by the arms and led him away. The room was instantly engulfed in an avalanche of noise, but Colon banged on the table and called for silence. He held a whispered conversation with Yakob Santos and Martino Vega, and then he addressed the gathering.

"We are as shocked," he said, "as everyone else by the revelations we have just witnessed. The proceedings against Senhor Dominguez are, of course, dismissed. Our sympathies go out to the Dominguez family, and if there is anything we can do to help you, we beg you to call on us at any time. This session of the Maamad is adjourned."

People crowded around Doña Angelica and Sebastian, everyone talking at once. But Sebastian asked them for a little time and privacy.

He leaned over to Doña Angelica. "Are you all right, Mother?"

She shook her head. "I'm not all right. I feel violated and sullied. I've never felt so humiliated or disgusted in my life. But don't worry about me. I'll be fine. That monster is wrong. He has not destroyed us. The shadow that has passed over our lives is gone. We will be fine." She dabbed at her eyes with a handkerchief. "I just need a few minutes alone."

210 · SCANDAL IN AMSTERDAM

"Of course, Mother," he said.

He went over to Rabbi Strasbourg and embraced him. Then he embraced Amos Strasbourg and wept openly on his shoulder.

"How can I ever —" he said.

Amos held up his hand. "Say nothing, my friend. Nothing needs to be said."

Sebastian felt a tap on his shoulder. He turned to face Miguel Castillo. His future father-in-law grasped Sebastian's hand and shook it.

"I sent Dulce home with her mother," he said. "This has been a terrible ordeal for her. An eighteen-year-old girl should never have to hear such monstrous things. But I stayed to speak with you."

Amos Strasbourg turned to leave, but Castillo put a hand on his arm to stop him. "You are Sebastian's friend, Senhor Strasbourg. There is nothing I am about to say that I cannot say in front of you."

"As you wish," said Amos Strasbourg.

"Sebastian, you are like my son," said Castillo. "You are not at fault in any of this. You were the victim of a horrible crime. I forgive the loan I made to you. You do not need to repay it. And I will help you get back on your feet again. You are a talented young man. We'll put all this behind us."

"I am sorry, Senhor Castillo," said Sebastian. "I gave you my word of honor that I would repay you, and I will not shirk from my obligation."

"Look at it as a wedding gift, a part of your dowry."

"I cannot, senhor. I thank the Almighty that this episode is over, but I cannot just turn the page and forget everything that happened. I made many mistakes, and I am responsible for them, even though I was lured into making them. With the help of the Almighty, I will repay the loan, senhor, every last guilder."

"I understand, Sebastian. It is a matter of honor. We can go into business together, and you can repay me little by little over a period of time."

Sebastian shook his head. "It is not so simple for me, senhor. I have to deal with this in my own way. I must make a break with the past and try to rebuild my life. I cannot do that in Amsterdam. You have a wonderful daughter, and you must find her a wonderful husband. But that husband will not be me. At this time, I cannot be the husband she needs and deserves."

Castillo was shocked. For a moment or two, he could not say anything. Then he bowed his head and nodded. "I understand what you're saying, Sebastian. I really do. I am sorry it has to end like this."

"So am I, senhor."

"You say you can't stay in Amsterdam," said Castillo. "Where will you go?"

"America," said Sebastian. "I am going to America. I own a piece of land in a colony called New Jersey. Maybe that will be the seed from which I can grow a new life for myself."

"America!" said Castillo. "But that is so far away."

"Yes, it is. It is the perfect place to make a new start."

"And I am going with you, Sebastian," said Amos.

Sebastian looked at Amos with astonishment. "But why?"

"Because I can also use a new start in a new place," said Amos. "And because you'll need a friend in America, and where will you find a better friend than me?"

Sebastian embraced Amos again.

"Amos, I just want —"

A sudden commotion in the hallway interrupted him. The door flew open, and Gonzalo burst into the hearing room.

"Don Sebastian," he said, "the constables took Setubal to his house for some things, and he never came out."

"What are you saying?"
"Setubal has escaped. He's vanished without a trace."

*To be continued …*

This volume is part of
THE ARTSCROLL SERIES®
an ongoing project of
translations, commentaries and expositions
on Scripture, Mishnah, Talmud, Halachah,
liturgy, history, the classic Rabbinic writings,
biographies and thought.

For a brochure of current publications
visit your local Hebrew bookseller
or contact the publisher:

# Mesorah Publications, ltd

4401 Second Avenue
Brooklyn, New York 11232
(718) 921-9000
www.artscroll.com

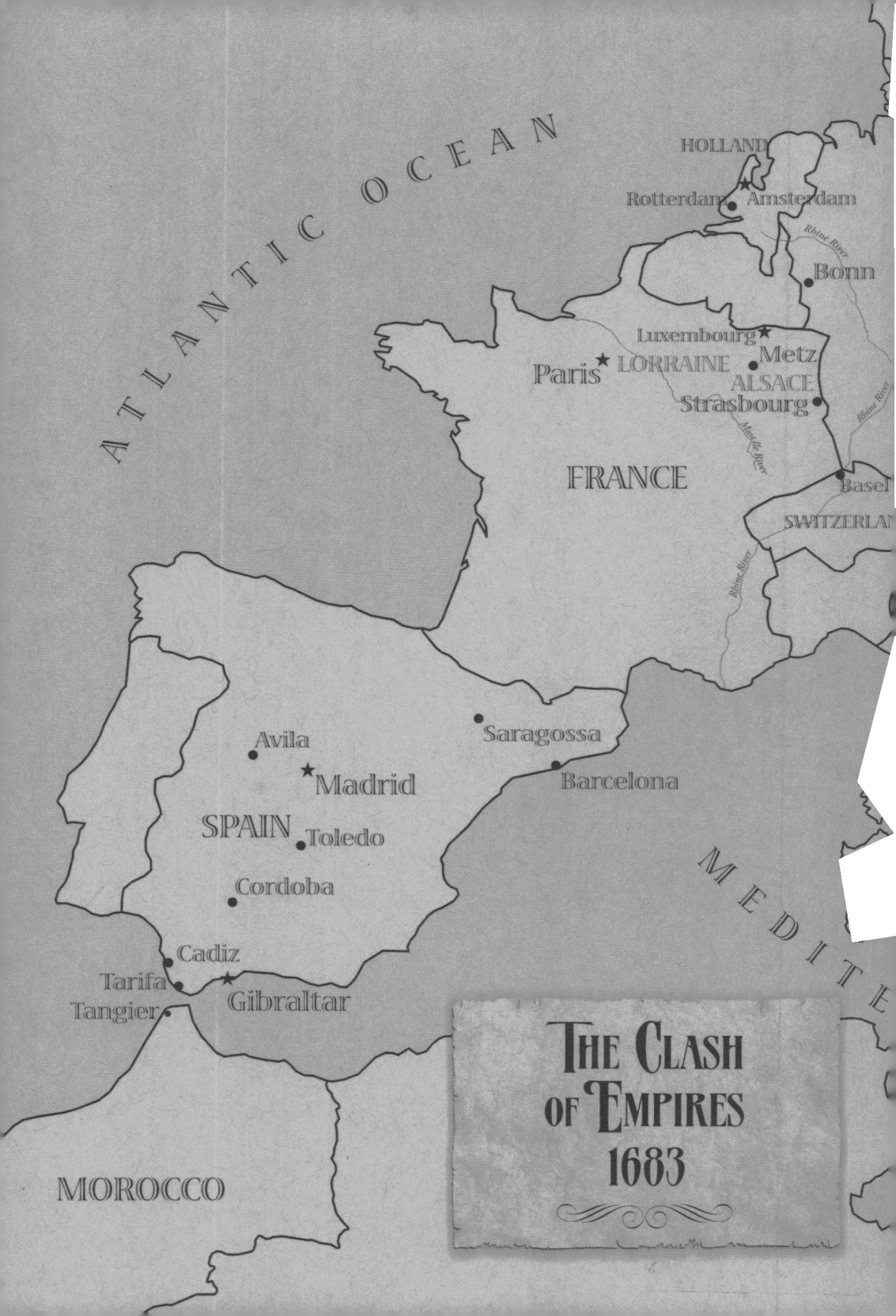

ATLANTIC OCEAN

HOLLAND
Rotterdam ★ Amsterdam

Rhine River

• Bonn

Luxembourg ★
LORRAINE  ● Metz
ALSACE
Paris ★  ● Strasbourg

Moselle River

Rhine River

FRANCE

● Basel

SWITZERLAN

Rhine River

Saragossa
●

● Barcelona

Avila
●    ★ Madrid

SPAIN  ● Toledo

Cordoba
●

Cadiz
●
Tarifa
● ★ Gibraltar
Tangier
●

MEDITE

MOROCCO

# THE CLASH
# OF EMPIRES
# 1683